RIPPED FROM
THE HEADLINES

VOLUME 12

THE CASTLE OF HORROR ANTHOLOGY

CASTLE BRIDGE MEDIA
DENVER, COLORADO, USA

CASTLE BRIDGE MEDIA
Denver, Colorado
Edited by Jason Henderson and In Churl Yo
Designed by In Churl Yo
Cover Illustration by andrey_l/Shutterstock.
This image has been modified.

This book is a work of fiction. Names, characters, business, events, and incidents are the products of the authors' imaginations. Any resemblance to actual persons, living or dead (or undead), or actual events is purely coincidental.

TABLE OF CONTENTS

Introduction...5

Frau Perchta Comes for the Count—*Leanna Renee Hieber*.....................8

Michael Collins on the Dark Side of The Moon—*Claire Low*.................25

Brew of the Bayou—*P. J. Hoover*...37

The Ghost Lake Mermaid—*Alethea Kontis*......................................61

Caretakers—*Will McDermott*...75

Ghost Chat—*Martin Ott*..92

Small Mercies—*Carmen Gray*..109

Paradice: A Gawain Story—*Charles R. Rutledge*............................119

Ghost Flight—*Dennis K. Crosby*..134

Sentient Slime—*Melanie Schubert*...156

INTRODUCTION

YOU KNOW THE FEELING. A headline flashes past – maybe it screams, maybe it just whispers – leaving behind a chill that digs in deeper than it should. We're drowning in information, aren't we? A constant flood of news, big events and small tragedies, piped straight into our pockets and living rooms. It makes the world feel… unsteady. Wired. Like something unsettling is waiting just off-screen. The stories you're about to read? They crawled out of that static, spun from the weird truths and dark maybe's hiding in the newsprint and the pixel glare. Horror ripped, sometimes still bleeding, right from the day's events.

But why reach for *more* fear when the real world dishes out plenty? It's an old question. We chase escapism, sure, even into the shadows of horror. But it's not just about looking away. Horror is a funhouse mirror – it twists and exaggerates, but it shows us something real about ourselves, our hang-ups, the ugliness we suspect hides in the neighbor's house, or even our own. Staring down fictional monsters in the safety of a story lets us get a handle on the real ones.

And let's face it, the real world feels particularly monstrous lately. The 24/7 news churn feeds anxiety like gasoline on a fire. Fake news deliberately muddies the waters. Deepfakes make you doubt your own eyes. Anonymous voices shout online until you don't know who or what to trust. Throw in a social climate that feels like a powder keg, and yeah, the ground feels shaky. What's real? What's manipulation? The lines get awfully blurry.

Still. We're here. We push through the noise, trying to find something solid. And that's where stories come in – maybe *especially* these kinds of stories. They dive headfirst into the darkness that headlines hint at, but they do something crucial: they remind us that truth, however buried, usually claws its way out. They show us what happens when the guardrails come down, when the lines we *thought* were clear get crossed. Exploring those grim 'what ifs' in fiction somehow helps us redraw the boundaries in reality.

In this volume, the Castle of Horror features editors have scoured cable, interweb, and social media feeds to source and assign a crack group of hot shot reporters to present to you their twisted lead stories filled with above-the-fold, all-caps horror for your reading pleasure.

Leanna Renee Hieber explores a shocking tale based on a chapter in her nonfiction *America's Most Gothic,* of a man who called himself a count, grave-robbing, and supernatural vengeance in "Frau Perchta Comes for the Count."

Claire Low gives us a look at an eerie incident that might have happened during Apollo 11 in "Michael Collins on the Dark Side of the Moon."

"Brew of the Bayou" by P. J. Hoover follows a group of friends whose spooky cocktail experiment takes a terrifying turn when they accidentally awaken an ancient swamp god.

Alethea Kontis' "The Ghost Lake Mermaid" and her best friend Jinna welcome a new ghost whose presence unravels the mysteries of Buckle Springs

"Caretakers" by Will McDermott tells the story of a traveling cat, one of many on a secret mission to serve and protect.

"Ghost Chat" by Martin Ott tells the story of a brilliant tech executive who develops an AI to mimic her late husband, to troubling results.

"Small Mercies" by Carmen Gray introduces us to the terrible crimes of New Orleans' legendary, haunted LaLaurie Mansion.

Inspired by one of the still unsolved cypher clues left by the Zodiac

Killer, Charles R. Rutledge's "Paradice" features Sir Gawain in the here and now, tracking a new series of murders and the terrible secret behind them.

In "Ghost Flight" by Dennis K. Crosby, a man's grief and a deal with a being capable of changing the very fabric of reality sets in motion the mystery of Malaysian Flight 370.

"Sentient Slime" brings us Melanie Schubert's icky-sweet and obsessive look at a scientist who saved Einstein's Brain and may be a little possessed by it.

Yes, these tales hold up a dark mirror to a chaotic world. But they're also proof that we need to make sense of it all, to process the scary stuff, to find our footing again. Think of them as echoes in the static – reminders that even when things look bleak in the news or online, the search for truth, for understanding, for that line between right and wrong... that fight continues. It has to.

Once again, Jason and I are thankful for the writing collected in this volume and the gracious authors who have shared their amazing talent with us, all of them unique voices from the genre's top writers. As always, thank you for supporting independent publishing, and please consider checking out the other volumes available from the Castle of Horror Anthology series for even more spooky stories. Oh, and also please support reputable journalists and news sources everywhere. Remember, the truth eventually will out – somehow, some way.

-30-

—In Churl Yo, publisher, Castle Bridge Media

FRAU PERCHTA COMES
FOR THE COUNT

By Leanna Renee Hieber

FOR ANY UNCONSCIONABLE ACT OF spiritual debasement and corporeal disrespect there is an equal and appropriate folklore to punish the perpetrator. But the old gods of any country, and their various officers, cannot be everywhere, and certainly not in each place where a diaspora may scatter.

And so it was that Augusta Grünwald, upon her death, volunteered herself as a spiritual representative of the Germanic tribes and watched over the goings on around the Key West, Florida cemetery to which she had tethered herself.

Matron of the graves since her death in 1890, she had decided at the time that rather than passing on, she'd be a better steward if she remained between worlds. Her position wasn't appointed nor elected among the dead, but she accepted the station with the seriousness one would expect from her people. It was now the 1930s and she had no intention of retiring.

Her family had been talented arborists for generations, her people descended from *Der Schwartzwald* and she prided herself on the fact that the Key West Cemetery over which she presided maintained healthy trees and thriving flowers. The atmosphere was quite different here than in the Black Forest, and as the twentieth century took a long breath after a terrible war that was hardly "Great," she was glad that her home country and her adoptive one were no longer, at least for the time, enemies. She found the new century baffling, but she was adapting. Her position had been a peaceful one. A benevolent watch.

Until 'the count' came to haunt the grounds.

Everything changed once a man claiming a title he did not own nor earn began to lord over the cemetery. Bearded, thin, middle-aged and walking with affect, the man who dubbed himself Count von Cosel had first entered the gates the night a young woman, much beloved by her Cuban family, was interred in a modest grave.

Elena Hoyos was neither this man's bride nor his relative. Yet he mourned as though she were his world. His galaxy. His grief seemed to know no bounds. This was Augusta Grünewald's first concern. Mourning was right and proper, but it should have its boundaries.

Augusta required details, so she listened in on neighborhood gossip.

"Only twenty-two," one neighbor clucked her tongue. "So young. Tuberculosis has no mercy."

"Who is this 'Count' von Cosel?" another neighbor asked one of the hospital orderlies who attended the funeral.

"The radiologist who treated her," the young man replied quietly. "His *real* name is Karl Tanzler. From Dresden, he's been in Key West for many years, acting like he's here on some sort of mission. When Elena Hoyos entered his X-ray room, he was a goner. Went mad for her."

A Hoyos relative joined in, quietly eyeing Tanzler with unease. "His methods went above and beyond, bringing equipment into her house, strange devices, demanding that her parents, all of us, comply with his orders. Unnatural."

Two immigrants from different backgrounds, patient and doctor, both trying to fend off death unsuccessfully.

Elena was a beautiful woman. Charming too. Augusta could understand anyone being taken with her. The young woman's ghost, luminous and slightly transparent, floated by.

Elena's spirit was making her rounds. Augusta had seen similar patterns unfold: the spirit may stare in wonder at the procession to the gravesite, gazing down at a casket with a contemplative mien before turning to behold family. Elena did this precisely, but then, with furrowed brow, looked at the man who had treated her in the hospital. She shook her head, puzzled, before floating back towards the hedgerow where Augusta watched. Elena's spirit did not speak with the living, perhaps she'd already tried, and this was one of her last rounds of goodbyes before she would go on toward her new adventures. Augusta knew the time might come when she too would go onwards toward a different assignment, but for now, she had a job to do.

Few people actually haunted their graves. Most haunted their haunts in life; the word *haunt* being suitable for the living and dead alike. Some might watch the sending off of their corporeal shell for their own closure. Others might be focused on friends and family, following in floating companionship to now and then smile when they were mentioned, or glimpsed with slight hope out of the corner of a living eye. They'd acknowledge their resting place but knew it was, as they were now; mere memory.

Elena noticed Augusta's silvery figure floating next to the oldest Cyprus tree in the cemetery and the young woman smiled at the elder shyly. Augusta lifted a hand in greeting. Not all dead wanted to speak to one another. Augusta always let the fresher ghost set the tone.

"How long will I remain so?" the young woman asked quietly, her pleasant voice carried the lilt of a Cuban accent. "Floating, finally free from pain?"

"As long as you wish," Augusta replied, her own German-accented English strong and precise, "if you concentrate hard to remain. But you do not *have* to. I stay because I enjoy greeting fellow travelers and watching over the stones, helping to keep order. What would make you happiest? Go and do that until your soul is so weightless that you float onto eternal bliss."

In the distance, a radio dial was turned higher. A Bolero carried softly across the verdant grass. Elena turned toward the rich, lush sound, opening her arms slightly, as if hoping to embrace the music. It was a sweetly sweeping Spanish-language tune, and the new ghost swayed gracefully in time with the music.

"I'd dance and sing forever if I could," she exclaimed. "That's what I've missed most."

"Then you should," Augusta encouraged. "Every spirit should follow their passion until the great light calls you onward."

The young woman brightened, her smile widened, as if someone had turned the key to a gaslamp higher and the flame of her spirit grew taller in the lantern.

Most spirits craved guidance. Permission. They were confused about what they were supposed to *do* if they found themselves still on this earthly plane. Because Elena had so missed activities of her healthier body, her spirit wanted one last dance, or many more. These simple delights could be held onto for as long as the spirit wished.

Elena's ghost waved at Augusta as she floated towards the music. One of the town's lively dance halls wasn't far, and Augusta hoped the familiarity of music and movement would transform the last physical memories of suffering into the transcendence that only leaving a body behind could offer.

While Elena moved on, friends and family exited the cemetery. The interring had long finished, but Augusta watched as the man who'd dubbed himself Count remained. He had commandeered a chair from the service and sat by the headstone, speaking quietly to the grave. It was no use trying to tell someone that their loved one wasn't there, below the ground, listening. Talking—even in abstract—to the loss itself was a critical part of the living's process. She let it be.

The one-sided discussion continued until it began to rain. Eventually, the downpour made him give up.

But night after night, he returned to mourn. Sitting and murmuring to the ground. Augusta found it odd, as no other family members were keeping such a consistent vigil.

As this self-appointed count examined the saturated terrain, he began to fret over the continuing storms. Rushing out of the gates, propelled by what seemed to be a surge of determination, Augusta realized something far more complicated was afoot. The "count," along with a Hoyos relative, returned, accompanied by gravediggers who began disinterring Elena's grave. If the cemetery sexton hadn't been with them, Augusta would have raised an alarm, creating as many sounds and moving things around the living that would frighten them away from their grim task. She'd foiled a few grave robberies in just such a manner. But this seemed sanctioned, however unorthodox. The young woman's damaged coffin was divulged, then hauled off by a distraught Tanzler. The ground around it gave way, leaving a wet, gaping mouth behind.

Unsure what to think until a mausoleum began to be built in its place, Augusta watched in fascination as the arched white stone sepulcher took shape. "The Count" spared no expense. While Elena's name was prominently displayed on the exterior, her body had also been freshly dressed and placed into a new, layered casket laid on a dais within, with a surrounding chamber large enough for a visitor to sit inside. The door was solid metal, fitted with several locks to which Tanzler had the only keys. Having assigned himself her guardian, and now that her body was no longer subjected to further deterioration in the muddy ground below, he then became her suitor.

"This is *not* how life and death are managed!" Augusta chided when he walked past. He almost turned. He almost heard her. She almost got through to him. But he shook his head, unlocked the three latches, and disappeared into the sepulcher. Elena's remains were now subject to absurd calling hours.

He held vigil at Elena's mausoleum, almost the whole night through, nearly every night, as if he were courting in her parlor. That he spoke to Elena as if she were alive revealed delusion. Augusta watched over these unprecedented proceedings with disapproval.

His appropriation of the title of count chafed Augusta; lies for the purpose of lording over others or affecting an idea of 'betterment' over the surroundings, all of it reeked of arrogance and reflected poorly on their people.

As a spirit, time was amorphous and unreliable; Augusta had no need of it, but she noted the dates changing on the newer headstones of the freshly dead and realized it had been two years since Elena had been re-interred. That Tanzler was there every night, well past the cemetery's stated hours, disturbed her. Did rules not apply to him? One night, she checked to make sure the casket inside the mausoleum remained undisturbed. Passing through the walls on a night she heard Tanzler snoring in his visitor's chair, she noticed how close he sat himself near the raised dais where her coffin lay. The coldness in Augusta's wake jolted Tanzler awake.

His eyes focused for just a moment then glazed over, catching then losing sight of her. Perhaps this stirred in him another otherworldly inclination. At some point in these deathly calling-hours, something changed about Tanzler and his approach, and it set Augusta on a new kind of guard. He began to exclaim from within the sepulcher, all in German. Which was of no use to Elena; the girl's living ear hadn't known *Deutsch*, though she was fluently bilingual in Spanish and English.

What Augusta overheard him exclaim *en Deutsch* made her furious. Anger afforded her enough spectral energy to rattle the metal tracery inside the mausoleum. Unfortunately, this only seemed to embolden Tanzler to think that Elena's spirit—and the spirits of the graveyard itself—were in agreement: He had to take Elena's body home with him.

He rushed out of the cemetery like a joyous child running towards a carnival tent. Augusta sickened, something began to churn within her, a dynamo, an engine that would power her forward through the unfolding events.

Within two days the madman struck, choosing a moonless night. Arriving in a wedding tuxedo, he hoisted Elena's coffin- the one he'd replaced her remains in after the first interring- onto a wheeled wagon and carted it towards the part of the cemetery gate that was most hidden from view of any homes, passersby or street traffic.

"Nein! Blasphemie!" Augusta cursed this offense; taking a body from its resting place for no discernable reason, unmooring the previously settled dead. She tried to float in front of him, to stop this, and for a moment his eyes seemed to focus on her. He smiled, suddenly radiant and joyful, as if thrilled for the company, perhaps thinking her an angel or some sort of heavenly host there to bless his actions rather than decry him.

He pressed past her, through her, making that churning roil of her spectral viscera spin faster. The echo of her own body was becoming a vortex of anger and disbelief. As Tanzler tried to hoist the coffin over the rear gate, with a rudimentary set of ropes, the entire casket tipped and fell onto him, a foul black liquid of rot dripping all over his pristine "wedding" attire.

Augusta remembered what it was like for her body to retch and her vaporous form heaved. She and Tanzler swore in German, hers a curse upon him, his a curse upon his luck.

But the curse had just begun, really.

Wherever this man was taking this body, the compact between the living and the dead had been broken. A sacred trust of life and death was entirely upended; dignity torn asunder.

As Tanzler wheeled the woman he loved- who clearly had no intention in life or in spirit of loving him in return- away from the cemetery and into the dark night, to God knows where, Augusta felt the air turn and open. Something ancient awoke and she welcomed it.

Opening her arms wide, she called out into the night, in the dialect of Old German her great grandmother used sparingly but effectively; bidding sleeping gods return.

When Augusta was a child in Stuttgart, a city at the edges of the Black Forest, a haven of old-growth trees and older-growth legends, her great grandmother regaled her of the ancient pagan forest guardians that the church had turned from heroes to horrors.

There was only one entity for the kind of debasement Augusta had just witnessed on sanctified ground, this kind of offense to their people had to be answered. Augusta was attuned to the woods, and she gathered close to a beautiful old pine, breathed it in, and prayed with ferocity, invoking a deity to cross the distances and mete out justice.

"Frau Perchta," Augusta murmured to the night. "Come collect this wayward son who brings shame to our people."

A yuletide entity who, in the darkest days of the year, would examine the deeds of mankind and dole out punishments accordingly, Frau Perchta hadn't always been a witch or a woman to be feared. Once, she'd been *Berchta*, the great shining one, a co-host of the wild hunt, protector of the forest and the spirits of the dead, particularly those who died young. But her role as great goddess had been turned inside out by the early church and she was transformed into something monstrous instead. If one was found lacking, Frau Perchta might slit open one's belly with a sharp implement; the converse of *Berchta* to whom expectant mothers would turn for protection.

"A god *should* be feared as well as adored," Augusta's great grandmother would murmur as she stared out the window of the cabin her family kept at the edge of the Black Forest, gazing into the inscrutable and too-dark shadows of that grand wood.

As Augusta, so many years later, stared into the darkness in the brush and thickets of the Key West cemetery, she thought of the happenstance that had brought her here. A series of family members depositing themselves on this island soil and encouraging others to join them here was a far cry from the old land and farther still from the old ways. But in this moment, the darkness between tall trees felt no different than her childhood in the Black Forest and her plea had indeed summoned the force she hoped for.

A lean, gaunt and shimmering form, shining and dark all at once, stepped out from a tree trunk. Her face was glowing like a spirit and her vaporous robes undulated outward as if they were ink spreading through water. Her appearance shifted back and forth between youth and age, maiden and crone, duality manifest. A bony hand clutched a tall staff that was alternately scythe-tipped and a shining star. Frau Perchta stepped out from the trees and suddenly, uncannily, she stood right before Augusta, gliding to her side in the instant.

"I have heard your spirit cry out, my child," the divinity said in the antiquated dialect that Augusta only understood because of her own ancestor's fondness for it. "What ails you so?"

"A man has broken the covenant between life and death. He is German, and he disgraces our people by his foul deeds and I felt only you could correct this grave mistake." Augusta explained what she'd witnessed in the cemetery, trying not to look Die Frau right in the glimmering eyes, as their pitch-black and shining abyss was so mesmerizing, Augusta felt she'd never be able to break free.

"All will bend to my hand in time." Die Frau reassured. "Keep watch." As quickly and liquidly as the divinity had approached, she retreated back to the pines of the cemetery grove.

Augusta did as instructed. But of course, Tanzler didn't return to the cemetery. He had no need to; he'd taken his respects with him.

"*How* do I keep watch?" Augusta asked the tall shadow between the trees that was always there if Augusta knew where to look. "I am rooted here, to this place he stole from."

"Are you, yourself, rooted?" Came a bemused voice as a silhouette blended into a pine trunk. "You tend trees but you are not one. If this desecration grieves you, *go*. Be my eyes and ears."

And just like that, Augusta found herself soaring; given the command, she followed orders. Like a bird, she glided high over rooftops until alighting along a nearby coastline, a pier pointing into the water like an accusatory finger. She sank towards the sandy bank, drifting down somewhere dark and deserted.

Drawn to a wooden shack with interior lanterns lit brightly, Augusta watched from a begrimed window for a moment before floating through the thin plank walls, into a modest space fit with odd equipment, a sputtering generator of some kind, and a body laid out in what Augusta could only describe as a paused state of decay. Elena, a semblance of her, lay on a slab, a still likeness of what Augusta had seen waft by in the cemetery before she floated free.

Tanzler spoke to the body as he washed it, in odd, sweet nothings and promises to revive her in some sort of ancient rite, all while trying to remove pieces of the burial gown that had become enmeshed with her skin. There was a long, coffin-like tank into which he placed her body and the electricity Tanzler had managed for this strange revivification process made the string of lights hung from wooden rafters flicker.

Augusta found her own form flickered with the lights, as they surged or guttered, so did she. In the cemetery there was no electricity and as she'd passed through the lines of current, so too had her energies become wound around the filaments of these lights and she could not break free. In horror, Augusta found that she could not leave this isolated cabin where a madman tried to raise the dead.

"Please," she murmured into the night, once Tanzer had exhausted himself and retreated to a cot near the tank. "Frau Perchta, help me. I may be your eyes and ears, but now tethered to this terrible place; bound to the lights and this horrible machine…"

A distant sound, like a stone scraping to sharpen a scythe, bid her turn her ghostly head towards the grove of trees along the coastline. The moon was bright across the water. A tall, darkly luminous silhouette stood between a willow and a palm.

"What is time, my child?" Frau Perchta whispered, her voice a death rattle. "Time for us is nothing. But for the wayward, like this man, time is a punishment. A sentence. He has committed a foul deed, that is certain, and it will be the end of him. The girl's spirit is not tethered there with you, she is free; you saw her go. You have decided this man and his acts matter, so it is up to you to make him fear you. I give you my blessing… Pull at the corner of his skin and someday, it may be years from now, he'll all come undone…"

And now Die Frau's scythe was in one hand, her needle of time in the palm of Augusta's other hand.

"It's simple, my child," Perchta instructed, with graceful, fluid motions. "Sweep." She motioned moving the scythe towards Tanzler, where its shadow fell over him. He involuntarily shuddered. "Stitch." Perchta made a looping motion with her other hand and as Augusta put the needle between thumb and forefinger, she folded her hand over in the air, jabbing and pulling. A miniscule drop of blood fell from Tanzler's side, onto the floor. "It will take the time it takes, my girl." And with that, Perchta retreated to the old world once more, leaving Augusta as her emissary.

Thusly, Augusta continued to keep watch over a man and the corpse he had dressed as his bride. Tanzler wanted to possess Elena, body and soul. He seemed oblivious to the fact that he was wholly unsuccessful in possessing the young woman's soul and focused his ministrations on her body. His treatment of Elena's remains, his treatment of Elena as an object, was what upset Augusta most. The business of a body, after death, was mere dust, carbon and rot. But the intentions around it were something else. *That's* where Tanzler had gone afoul. A cause for damnation was trying to *own* someone else's remains. To deny the autonomy of rest.

And yet, years passed in this manner. The body's decay gave way to something else, a sort of pickling, and Augusta was glad her sense of smell had faded with her own corporeality. But as the remains transformed, so did Augusta's understanding of her purpose; the pure gratification of becoming the shadow of doubt that lurked at the corner of a pompous man's eye. *Sweep. Stitch.* She was embodying the dread that served as the engine for all harrowing tales and cautionary texts.

A day came when the constant proximity of workers who had been sent to restore the pier below drove Tanzler from the property. As the generators stopped, the spark that was Augusta's form was finally untethered and she flew free. Or, at least, so she thought. The spark of electricity that had become wound through the coil of her soul re-wrapped itself to the life force of this lie of a man. Through just so many stitches.

"Damn it all," Augusta murmured. She was now stuck with this abomination. But, she reminded herself, there was more to witness and she had pledged to keep watch.

His eccentricities not to be outdone, he secretly enclosed the coffin in the most baffling thing. Inexplicably, Tanzler was in the possession of a small, unflyable aircraft. Into this cockpit he had Elena's casket stowed, and had the whole affair towed to a new location. She overheard him murmuring to the casket that he'd get the aircraft going someday, to send them to the stars; where Elena could be resurrected by radiation from space. Augusta almost laughed at the preposterous notions but was sobered by the fact that these remains had no say in the matter, absurdity or no.

In another sad, wooden-frame shed where a hand-painted sign read *Von Cosel's Laboratory,* the cycle began again.

But this time, as more years passed, a fresh layer of wax was added to the husk of Elena's body, a new note of decay hung in the air, and the last of any moisture in the tissues was desiccated to dust. The transformation from remains to fabrication was almost entirely complete. Only bones remained. The corpse, now a grotesque caricature, had become so far removed from Elena that Augusta could finally begin to sow the seeds she had promised the great, shining *Berchta* she would plant.

Punishment was a harvest; a cycle that continued to be gathered by the repeated sweeps of a sharp scythe.

When her righteous fury rose, each day Augusta swept her hands over him and the shadow of the scythe made its mark. Any time he engaged with the mannequin remains, a droplet of blood was collected, wicking away.

As all unholy things must eventually rear their head, the day came when Tanzler's actions were revealed.

A relative confronted Tanzler. Elena's sister demanded to know why the mausoleum in the cemetery had become so overgrown and untended. She suspected the worst. When Tanzler simply invited the woman in to see how well he had been treating her sister, a new layer of hell opened up. Augusta wished she could have shielded Elena's family from the indignities of that humble dwelling, but the body was revealed nonetheless, in a sordid bridal gown, the room smelling of too-strong soaps and perfumes. But nothing could fully mask the decay. Or the sister's horror.

Now, the insult to Elena's remains had been broadened to include the shock and disgust of the living. It was another strike against Tanzler's soul to reveal this defilement as if it were an honor, another affront to the gods that governed him. And soon, police came calling with a warrant for his arrest, per unlawful removal of a body and defilement of a grave. Tanzler appeared shocked by this; confused as to why anyone would see what he had done as anything other than a great service, his reality so entirely opposite to everything and everyone around him.

An arrest, a charge, several nights in prison and then a trial.

Through it all, Augusta was like a pennant; floating and billowing behind Tanzler in this flurry of activity that unfolded. The resentment about being now tethered to this man, rather than to the cemetery she'd chosen to haunt, had now fully given way to the duty of lurking at the corner of his eye to instill dread while she continued her tasks.

Sweep. Stitch.

Perhaps it was the unbelievable nature of it, the stranger-than-fiction aspect of Tanzler's theft of, then recreation of, Elena's body that made him into an overnight celebrity. The story was covered in newspapers all across America, copies of which made their way to Tanzler's cell.

Augusta watched it all in a montage of activity, her spirit-senses too overwhelmed to be cognizant of every moment. A time-slip was the only way she could stomach the entirety.

This spotlight, in its own way, protected him. Augusta's efforts and Die Frau's powers combined couldn't come collect him, not in such a public place. Perchta was still an old-world creature that relied on the hushed concern of children, the misapprehension of her enormity and the deepest of shadows in which to move.

During the trial, Augusta floated in the corner, scowling at the too-packed courthouse while the deluded defendant, wearing a suit coat and tennis shoes to a courthouse where he defended his right to a corpse bride, insisted he did nothing wrong. That he was entirely sane.

Letters arrived calling this man a romantic. Augusta felt ill; was her own world so unrecognizable? Was she, now, one of the old gods after all, befuddled by American sentiment? Where did she belong, if such an act as this was not soundly and universally decried? Could her soul return to Germany? No. Something ugly rose there too, something her fair-minded ancestors who fought for democracy in the 1848 revolution would have stood against now. She was stuck with this abomination. In their shared new country.

As baffled as the judge seemed by the entire circus before him, the limits of the law were clear. The statute of limitations on the desecration of a grave had lapsed. The count was free to go.

A bit of justice in the world remained, thankfully, in that Tanzler was denied his request to have Elena's husk returned to him.

"But what of the punishment?" Augusta murmured, watching as he left the courthouse, a quiet entourage following him. He returned to his sad shack of a home and gave tours of his equipment and Elena's death masks. He started writing aggrandizing memoirs as the last of his funds began slipping away. Augusta tracked it all with growing frustration.

Closing her eyes, she turned inward to the being whose powers she had summoned and swallowed as if they were a hot coal in her belly. "Berchta," Augusta murmured reverently. "Where is the punishment? To tear at his skin, to split him open…"

"Yes, daughter," a voice from within answered. "You have and you will."

Censure would take the time the goddess had promised it would take; the timeline was not Augusta's to determine. She comforted herself with the knowledge that even though it felt like Tanzler had been given too long to live in continued unreality, that the shadow of Frau Perchta had been long on his doorstep. The man squinted nervously into the corners, staring too long at Augusta as she floated amidst the scrub outside his 'laboratory doors'. She increased her labors.

Sweep. Stitch.

Once Tanzler had milked all he could from his infamy, he said goodbye to Key West, and the Cemetery, by blowing up Elena's mausoleum. The violent, final act of a petulant child. If he could not have Elena's remains then nothing would remain to remember her by. And that, in the end, was perhaps the saddest aspect, that there was no grave marker for Elena, or her sundry parts. They'd all been folded in on themselves in a little box, deposited in the dead of night by the cemetery sexton who would take the spot to his own grave. Augusta knew where the ground held the girl's bones while her spirit remained long departed. Nothing called Elena back to that patch of earth; she was out dancing in eternal moonlight.

Augusta was there, of course, when the explosion happened in the cemetery. Her incorporeality made her unable to stop the act, but she stood near enough to absorb some power from the blast. This was enough for the final act to begin; curtains closing slowly over Tanzler with each hollow beat of his prideful heart.

His material conditions having continued to wither, it was in an out of the way, unkempt abode in which Tanzler tried to resurrect the efforts of the past decade. Trying to breathe life into a mannequin, he recreated another effigy of Elena, using one of her death masks and rebuilding her funeral bier turned marriage bed, a reliquary of delusion.

But he knew, by then, that something was coming for him and had been for some time. It was not there to applaud his efforts nor his shrine. It was weighing his soul.

Each day had become emptier than the day before.

He began to hear the sweep of the scythe and the whisper of the thread as the two actions began to take shape.

It wasn't until the last breaths of his misspent life that Augusta fully understood the goddess' busywork.

Sweep. Stitch. Tie the knot.

As Tanzler's body fell to the floor, in the throes of death itself, that's when he finally *saw* what he'd thought was some divine encouragement. His eyes widened in horror, focusing fully on the guise of whatever Perchta wanted him to see, either bright and shining or dark and terrible, full of duality, the face of judgement is best reserved for the guilty to see.

Now, daughter, a voice rumbled inside Augusta, *snip the last thread and let it all come apart...* Augusta's hands were claws and with one click of her talons, suddenly all the sweeping cuts of the scythe that she'd been passing over his form actualized.

His body was sliced into thousands of pieces, stretched out in a long line of frozen, hollow moments, a terrible garland of viscera held together by the stitches of his sins. Each sliver of his corpse held a moment in time that fully revealed him interacting with wax and cloth, plaster and wire. *Not* a person, *not* a spirit. That which he'd crafted was full of emptiness after all.

This was a certain hell. A parade of desolate moments when the illusion is laid bare and there is nothing left but the lifeless truth. He was held, there, his purgatory pulled apart in a winding entrail of loneliness. He did not, in the end, own that girl. He did not possess her and never had. The slices of his hands held only dust and always had, from the moment her spirit floated off dancing. He had died alone with only a puppet. Rotting within his rotten acts, he now lay in disintegrating stasis until the synapses melted away.

In that moment, as Augusta stared down at the putrefying array, she knew she was again free.

In a rippling, shuddering effect, a shadow separated itself out from the wall.

Frau Perchta stood, alternating between the shining one, beautiful Berchta, and the tall, lean creature that led The Wild Hunt. When Augusta began to bow her head, Frau reached out a long fingernail and kept Augusta's gaze focused on her onyx, endless pools of her eyes where all of life's mysteries swirled in a dizzying lurch.

"Have I honored you?" Augusta asked quietly. "I fear I was not swift enough-"

"See it as I see it, daughter," Die Frau halted her, waving her bony hand. "Time, and we, are liminal beings. See it as it unfolded. I protect the souls of the young dead."

Suddenly they were back in the cemetery where Augusta had first summoned Perchta.

"If one of my children errs in such a way as this, we're the gods who must answer for him. I made it our responsibility, not that child's burden. She is free. *We* took up the yoke. And we'll pass this terrible tale along to others. Not to memorialize. But to shame. This thread will find its way out into the world. It will find another soul that will stitch him into his lonely hell all the tighter. Caught in the threads of his own reconstructions."

"You've done well, Augusta Grünwald," Perchta continued, her luminous face a maiden one moment, a regal old woman the next. "Your *nachname* may mean green forest, but your people learned their arts from the *Black* Forest and all the magic therein. Do you wish to return there now, to *Der Schwartzwald?* You called me here but I can take you home."

Augusta shook her head. "Thank you, but this is home now. It needs watching over. People need to be reminded to respect one another, alive and dead. And those of us who have come here from afar need to remember that we have not been relinquished of our duties to the old gods of our lands."

"Then keep watch, good Augusta. Tell our stories. And when another German woman is affronted by these indignities, she'll take up your mantle and you'll have earned yourself a rest."

And so, this storyteller takes up the yoke. She urges others to clean, tidy and mend their souls, for the sake of all spirits.

And what of Elena?

Again, as all the old magics do, this tale must return to the power of the name.

Elena means a shining light.

Berchta means the exact same. The shining one, as she always did, shepherds the innocent who die too young.

So does that gentle, youthful spirit join the old goddess now and then, dancing on the edges of forests, through the dualities of time, turning a blinding, obliterating, outshining and outlasting light against all who would make such a mockery of death.

#   #   #

Author's Note

While Augusta Grünwald is a fictional character created as the 'watcher' over this sordid tale, everything she presides over actually happened. Karl

Tanzler really did live with a corpse bride for nine years. The rot on his 'wedding outfit', his 'reconstruction' of the body, proudly showing the poor sister of Elena Hoyos her wax-covered corpse, the little airplane he hoped to send to space, the trial, the findings, her secret reburial; *all* of it really happened. We'll be writing about it in *America's Most Gothic: Haunted History Stranger than Fiction* and The Haunted History Chronicles has a great episode about the whole situation.

Frau Perchta really is an old Germanic deity who became 'rebranded' as a witch, as described, but became more associated with the darker side of the holidays (a la Krampus) per the church's condemnation of her worship practices. Perchta's feast day is Epiphany Eve.

My German ancestors immigrated to America in the late 19th century, and they would be, like I've been, appalled at this story, so I brought something of their era into this tale, in hopes of dispensing justice and punishments that were never served.

MICHAEL COLLINS ON THE DARK SIDE OF THE MOON

By Claire Low

"YOU WILL BE THE LONELIEST person in human history."

"That's right, doc," I say patiently. One of NASA's attempts to habituate me to the upcoming mission was to pair me with a shrink to help me withstand the psychological pressures of Apollo 11. Except this guy is a little too earnest, a bit too 'aw shucks,' a tad overawed about the situation. He straightens his glasses.

"I mean it, Michael. I want you to try and let the feeling sink in right now, so it doesn't hit you all at once when you're out there: three billion humans, every living soul, on planet Earth and you, something like 186,000 miles away, looking down on them. Neil and Buzz out of radio reach for a good 47 minutes per rotation every time you reach the dark side of the Moon. Nobody, and I mean nobody, to talk to except yourself. It's intimidating even for the strongest minds."

I hold up my hands in an *I surrender* gesture. "I get it, doc. You know, I enjoy my own company." I attempt a shrugging, devil-may-care attitude. Maybe this can be my last session with the shrink. The ink blot tests, I'd had far too much fun with them, to be perfectly honest.

"Enjoy your own company, do you? Well, I'm glad to hear it," the young psychologist says. "Just breathe with me now."

He takes a few gushy, showy breaths; he is a little snotty, a little gurgly, like a drain. I try and match his breaths while stifling a chuckle at his dying fish impression.

"Picture the vast emptiness. The great void. Being completely, utterly alone."

I breathe politely along with him. This brings in the stale popcorn smell of his office. Soon, there will be thousands of miles between me and him.

"Very good, Michael."

I grin at him, unable to suppress the urge to wind him up. It's my contrarian streak. All my years as a fighter pilot couldn't train it out of me.

"You know, doc?"

"Yes, Michael?"

"What if I see something out there? What if I'm not alone?"

His young eyes get a bit bigger and sadder and I could kick myself, knowing I've just guaranteed myself at least another two sessions with this dork.

"Oh, Michael. No. You will be."

\#   \#   \#

Being the so-called 'third man' isn't the most glamorous role, but hey, a heist isn't much good without a getaway driver. Armstrong and Aldrin need a ride home and I am mission critical. Besides, a pilot's gotta pilot. It's what I love, have loved ever since I was a kid watching Buck Rogers and Flash Gordon adventures, which sent my mind spinning into orbit, dreaming of voyages to Mars. I'm here because I can withstand vibration, high temperatures, isolation, darkness and heat. While the link up has a fair bit of pressure on—quite a lot of pressure, it must be said, since the most nightmarish scenario involves President Nixon announcing the death of two astronauts—flying about before then, well, honestly it's a piece of cake. I'm thinking I'll play a little music, have a coffee, maybe get a little shuteye.

\#   \#   \#

With the landing module having detached, sending Buzz and Neil down to the ivory orb in the sky, the silence is rather refreshing. I hear none of Aldrin's snoring, none of Armstrong's corny music on the tinny radio. NASA's overly paternalistic attempts at pastoral care had been overkill; I would never have made it as a fighter pilot without a steely core, a locus of control, a firm stoicism.

Earth, my home planet, is a bright, banded marble rolling about in the inky black expanse of space. Being able to hold up a thumbnail and cover all humans currently alive, it's the darnedest feeling, a little godlike, I would say. I snap some pictures and a jolt of electricity surges through me, like my veins are humming with exultation. I am one of very few humans to ever travel beyond the limits of Earth's atmosphere. I am a finely honed tool, a machine. My limits have been tested; I have been whittled like a blade to end up here. There is no one quite like me.

On the second pass around the dark side of the Moon, something else surges through me. Dread, paranoia, only for a fleeting second – but I breathe, and it passes (hey, the shrink was right). Still, the feelings creep up again, like one of those awful pop-up dolls in a music box. Stuff it back down and it's ready to reemerge, with teeth. I am meant to be alone. Truly alone-alone, literally the loneliest. Why, then, do I feel there are eyes on me? That's insane, I remind myself. Come on, Mike. I chuckle and then, wouldn't you know it, drift off to sleep.

#   #   #

I awaken to a clatter, the sound of a hatch being moved. Goddamn, something had better not have come loose. Aldrin is always forgetting to keep everything properly fastened and stored away; I'd warned him that he'd eventually get smacked in the eye by his own floating toothbrush. And if not something like that, perhaps something needed an easy repair. The alternative was a bit too grim to contemplate.

#   #   #

The shape of another man emerging out of a hatch is not something I was expecting to see; it was the least likely thing I could have predicted. He unfurls himself and he is familiar, creepily familiar. He has my height, he has my silhouette, he has the same NASA high-performance, military-style clothing. He is coming closer.

I'm dreaming. Hallucinating. I have lost blood flow to my brain. Or, perhaps, far too much blood is flooding my brain. It's another man, in fact, another me.

Within close range, we regard each other. He is exactly me, as far as I can tell, the lights being what they are out here, and microgravity being what it is. Astronauts will tell you about 'astronaut vision' – in short, you've got to get along with compromised eyes, like someone sorely in need of corrective lenses. You train for this. And so, I peer at the man, and he peers at me. And from what I can make out, he is more Michael Collins than I am. Sure looks like he, annoyingly, is slightly handsomer. He lacks the acne scars on my face and his teeth are nicer, a bit straighter, a bright ribbon of white that slightly glows at me. They have an uncut air about them, from disuse – like they have never bitten into a rare steak or a hard apple, nor beef jerky nor corn on the cob; they are a little sharp. And, for some reason, one of his hands is in his pocket.

He continues to move through the pressurised air as though born for this purpose; he glides. He is closer now, a little too close. He is at a range more familiar to actors in prom night teen movies, about to go in for a goodnight kiss. His smell is a little briny, a little like a jar of pickles. The animal side of my brain awakens from its slumber, and begins to scream in protest at the wholly unnatural sight of what could only be described as a bizarre, shocking twin – for I had certainly been born alone and was expecting to die alone. I suppress it. I am, after all, highly trained. I stuff a hot flare of rage back down.

"May I help you, sir?"

"They told me I would be alone." The Other Michael's voice is identical to mine but it has the edges sanded off, no accent. It is the elevator music version of mine.

"Funny you should say that, they said the same thing to me," I say. A chuckle comes out before I can stop it. Obviously, I am dreaming. Obviously, I have detached from reality entirely. I run my hand over my chin and as though unable to help himself, The Other Michael does the same thing. This action triggers the animal side of me again. In the weird, unnatural copy I see my own most-hated aspects of myself. I feel something for him, a surge of potential violence. This, too, must come back down.

"Who are you?" I ask.

"Michael Collins," the copy says, offering a hand.

Through force of habit, I grip the copy's hand firmly and shake it, thinking this is the most fucking strange moment of my life thus far. "Michael Collins," I say right back. "And where did you come from? And how long have you been hiding in here? And do Buzz and Neil even know about you?"

Fact of the matter is, everything in this command module is counted and weighed down to the very last gram. Only mission-critical items are allowed on board, so The Other Michael – if he is here, if he isn't a figment of my brain detaching from reality – is here under NASA's specific auspices. He's here because he's meant to be.

"I'm a perfect copy of you, specifically a clone made of your DNA, powered by artificial intelligence," The Other Michael says.

"What?" I say. "That's a pretty gross violation." The Other Michael smiles blandly in response. He floats there, floating as I float, our eyes locked together. I think back to orientation, the physical examinations, the swabs and blood samples. They have enough DNA to make an army of Michaels. I'm insistent. "I did not consent to this."

Here, he adopts a falsely cheery demeanor that is, somehow, worse than open hostility.

"Michael, you did. Page 609 of the paperwork. Remember?"

Ah, yes, the paperwork. It had been more onerous than reorganising a filing cabinet and duller, too. Eventually I just put my John Hancock everywhere it had to go.

The Other Michael continues on. "You get it, right? If anything happened to you and you did not return to Earth in one piece, it would be a political nightmare for the Nixon administration. Got to have a back up.

There's no way you, Armstrong and Aldrin won't return to Earth. This is what it takes."

To see if he'll imitate me again, I put both my hands behind my head. He starts to copy me, but catches himself, leaving one hand in his pocket.

"Something wrong with that hand?" I say, nodding at it.

The Other Michael smiles and the smile is eerily bland. He smiles like someone who understands the facial expression from having read about it, or being briefed about it once, as in his teeth rise in his face in the manner of the sun rising over a mountain. It is not beautiful, though. He withdraws his hand slowly, as though he's making a fetish of it. Like a weird striptease.

"Six fingers? That's it?"

The copy shrugs. "Thought it might bother you."

"I don't have six fingers on one hand."

The copy, a little coldly, says, "Well. Congratulations."

"Why is this the only aspect of me – I mean you – that's not a perfect replica?"

"Artificial intelligence has trouble with hands. The one thing it has trouble rendering."

"Huh. Well, OK then. Say, I wonder if you have my memories as well as everything else of mine. Who did we have a crush on in high school?"

"Donna Reed?" the copy says hopefully.

"Wrong."

"Huh."

"What's the use of you, anyway?" I say to The Other Michael. "I'm still here and they obviously don't need two of us."

"I don't know," the copy admits and I can tell he's being honest. "I was supposed to activate upon your total destruction or incapacitation."

"And I am neither dead nor destroyed."

"So it would seem," he agrees.

We regard each other for a moment, we take each other in. May as well deal with it, I suppose. May as well try and get along with my new twin. I guess they used the same specifications for the suit I'm in, I guess he was good to go. This is a two-for-one deal. He's probably in even better condition than I am. I mean, my body isn't quite what it used to be. Wasn't so very long ago that they fixed a loose disc between two cervical vertebrae, and patched me up using a little chunk of bone from my hip. The copy, I suppose, is a mint condition baseball card of a human. If you can call him that.

I fix The Other Michael with an even stare. I rearrange my face into what I hope is a genial expression. "We could make the best of it, I suppose. Here, why don't we do some tasks together? I'm the third man, you're the fourth man. Why not make this the most productive mission ever?"

He says, quietly, "I'm the third man."

"What?"

"Nothing," he replies. "What shall we do first?"

There are a few things on my to-do list, but compared to the importance of the link up later, the one that will fetch Buzz and Neil off the Moon and deliver them back to Earth, they amount to little more than busywork. I've got my orbiting experiments to do; lots of monitoring; I can measure background radiation; measure distances; take photographs. Not much to write home about, y'know. Compared with 'Man Walks on Moon', 'Collins Takes A Few Pictures' isn't such a great headline.

"How about some photographs?" I suggest. I lead the way to where the camera is stashed and as we go, I look at those teeth of his, the bright ribbon of teeth in his face. Is there enough food on board for another person? Has to be, right? But he's only meant to be here upon me having gone, so maybe they didn't add provisions for a fourth person. He looks back at me and I wonder if he's thinking the same thing.

I hand him the camera and he takes a few pictures of Earth in a perfunctory sort of way; the sight of our home planet doesn't seem to move him much. Instead, he's much too drawn to me. The Other Michael stores the camera and smiles again, that awfully vacant smile. It reminds me of the falsely cheery Christmas windows of failing electronics stores downtown – lights are twinkling but there's nothing really to be happy about.

"I just cannot fight this feeling, Michael," he says.

"...what feeling?"

"They said I would be alone. And I'm not. But I was supposed to be."

He does not stop smiling as his hand comes up to my throat. It comes up far faster than I would have thought possible in the microgravity inside the module. To move around in here feels like a bit like scuba diving. His deftness is unexpected.

With a magnificent grip strength that reminds me of a state bouldering champion, he calmly blocks off my airway. Blackness swims in and out of my field of vision. I have just enough time to think of how odd it will be if my last conscious thought is of my own face, an uncanny version of it, looming over me. Already, the lights are going out. Blood vessels are bursting, gaskets are blowing in my brain. All the while, the pain is searing, burning through me, my very cells are on fire, my body is screaming that it wants to live.

In this moment, my mind reaches for something, a life raft in the ocean. My mother's face looms up before my eyes. She's so real.

I'm dying, I'm dying.

Then—another thought: how is it possible he's stronger than I am? We are made of the same things. Identical raw materials, practically. Except I'm powered by a genuine human heart and he is powered by algorithms, the scrappy pieces of me make me exceptional where he is bland, I can hurt more than he can, have survived so much more than he has, and that's because I am, by far, the better Michael Collins.

He has nothing to live for, but I do.

Adrenaline surges through me, temporarily erasing the pain. I force my arms up between his, twist my face towards his hands, with great urgency, and bite down. Success. He is forced to release me. A bloodied finger – the extra one, incidentally – comes off in my mouth. I spit it out, like hawking the greatest loogie in the history of loogies. My mouth is filled with a metallic taste. The bitten-off finger, if you can believe it, soars away through the module and manages to hit the play button on Neil's goddamn cassette player and Sonny and Cher start up their syrupy crooning.

Babe.

I got you babe.

"Yaaarrghh," I roar as if the music has personally goaded me. At least I remember this from the first aid protocol training: blood, in space, isn't necessarily about to gush into the air and fly away. The surface tension of the droplets – of any liquid, really – relative to the body will cause the droplets to remain on the body, at least, to a certain extent. And thank God for that, I just don't want any instruments all clogged up by a bleeding, now ten-fingered clone.

#   #   #

The Other Michael Collins and I are then locked into the worst and most murderous space ballet that ever was set to Sonny and Cher. He's in pursuit of me, I'm in pursuit of him, he's completely dogged, he's on me, I'm on him. He's after me like an utterly single-minded space maniac, and I realize, then, that this is in fact a description of me, too. I have all my life been an utterly single-minded space maniac. We really are each other.

Trouble is, when objects bang together in weightlessness, there is no anchoring. We rotate in pitch and we rotate in yaw around each other as we try and force our hands to attack each other, we have no weapons, and we cartwheel together through the module. We sure as shit aren't going to work together anymore.

Right then, another lunge forward. He's fast, he strikes in the manner of a cobra and I have my hands up near the sockets of his eyes, perhaps the weakest part of him and… and… I scoop.

His eyeballs are in my hands, the horrible, slippery reality of them and ugh, disgusting, first the finger, now the eyes. Wanting to avoid another body-parts-floating-away incident I shove them inside a Velcro-fastened pocket of my suit. *What big eyes you have…*

I assume this has disarmed him, but relentlessly, in the manner of a zombie, he continues to pitch and roll forward, much more clumsily, to where he assumes I am.

Seeing 'myself' with scooped-out eyes, well, it's not a sight I'll be forgetting anytime soon. He bleeds from the voids where his eyes used to be, but like his finger wound, the blood sort of just beads there.

"Michael?" he says, eerily calm. "Michael?" Like he hopes I'll respond to help him locate me, like we're little kids playing Marco Polo.

I swim through the module as carefully and silently as possible, bringing

33

with me a brown tether with clips on either side. Its designated purpose is a footrest for Neil, but I have other plans.

Trusting that the element of surprise will work to my advantage, I pull the tether tight about the copy's neck, and though he keeps almost floating away and moving about, I've got him, I've got him like a me-shaped balloon. That windpipe of his, a facsimile of my own, it's getting crushed down, and he kicks, he tries to struggle away from me but unlike me, perhaps, he has no mother to summon, no one he loves to come to him when he needs them the most and maybe this is why within a few minutes, he goes limp and ceases his struggles.

I use power cables to fasten him to himself, hands to legs, folding him up like a folding chair, all the while rolling in pitch and yaw. It takes quite a bit of effort, but I find a spot for him. I stuff him into a briny-smelling hatch, limbs jammed in everywhere, reminding me of how I can never quite refold a map the way it originally was. The last thing to stuff away is his head and it's awful and also, awfully convenient how I can get my fingers into those emptied-out eye sockets, like holding a bowling ball, and this helps me force the last of him down. Eyeless and crumpled, he is still so much like me that it hurts to look at him, it rings this wretched bell inside me, sirens, alarms, the works go off in my brain and I must gather myself even as a bit of regret settles in: what have I done?

For about a minute, I take a few gigantic rattling breaths like the shrink told me to.

#   #   #

With the Moon no longer blocking its signal, the radio abruptly crackles back to life.

"Columbia, this is Houston. Do you read? Over."

My mouth is dry, my tongue a ragged corn husk of a thing. I run it around my teeth.

The radio insists: "Columbia to Houston, do you read? Over."

Finally, I clear my throat and my voice returns. "Houston, this is Columbia. Over."

It's strange – my voice sounds a little different to my ears. Then again, space has a way of changing nearly everything about you. Getting used to being back on Earth can be the hardest part.

The guy in Mission Control, his relief is audible. "Christ, Mike, what happened to you? You hardly sound like yourself. You coming down with something?"

I pause for a beat, clear my throat one more time. "I feel fine."

#   #   #

Author's Note

An ABC obituary for Apollo 11 astronaut Michael Collins, the oft-forgotten third man on that pioneering mission to the Moon, describes his total isolation from all of humanity and long stretches in which he could not even talk to Buzz Aldrin or Neil Armstrong. While thinking of the mental toughness required for this complete and brutal solitude, I realized – it would be terrifying if he wasn't alone after all.

Sources

Jordan Hayne, *As Michael Collins drifted above the Moon, he held a 'secret terror' for the Apollo 11 mission*, Australian Broadcasting Corporation, www.abc.net.au/news/2021-04-29/michael-collins-apollo-11-mission-secret-terror/100103584, published April 29 2021, accessed in December 2024.

NASA Johnson Space Center Oral History Project, Edited Oral History Transcript, Michael Collins Interviewed by Michelle Kelly, Oakville, Ontario, Canada – October 8, 1997. Michael Collins Oral History. Accessed in December 2024.

Jeffrey Kluger, *Apollo 11 Had 3 Men Aboard, But Only 2 Walked on the Moon. Here's What it Was Like to Be the Third*, Time magazine, time.com/5624528/michael-collins-apollo-11/, published July 11, 2019, accessed in December 2024.

Andrew Chaikin, A Man on the Moon: The Voyages of the Apollo Astronauts, Viking, 1994.

James R. Hansen, *First Man: The Life of Neil A. Armstrong*, Simon & Schuster, 2005.

60 Minutes Australia, Remembering Apollo 11 Astronaut Michael Collins, YouTube, uploaded three years ago, youtube.com/watch?v=XzAFzsJ0l-w.

Special thanks to Dr Brad Tucker, Astrophysicist and Cosmologist, the Australian National University.

All errors are the author's own.

BREW OF THE BAYOU

By P. J. Hoover

"HEY, YOU THINK I CAN hit that gator with my beer can?" Jake asked. He pulled back his arm, ready to launch the Bud can deep into the marshland of the Florida swamp.

Mia wrestled the can from his grasp—a feat not too difficult given that the empty can he was holding was the eighth he'd downed in the last two hours. "Don't mess with the gators, idiot," she said.

Jake twisted around, trying to grab the can. "Don't you see the way he's looking at me?" he slurred. "I swear he's watching me."

"Trying to decide if you'd taste better with mustard or barbeque sauce," Simone said.

"Definitely barbeque sauce," Alex said, stepping out the front door of the cabin onto the porch. "Everything is better with barbeque sauce. Speaking of which…"

"Please tell me dinner is ready," Simone said. "My stomach sounds like mountain lions are having a party in there."

Alex leaned down, placing his ear to Simone's stomach. His eyes went wide. "More like cave trolls. Now let's eat." He walked back into the cabin, not casting the gator another glance.

But Mia couldn't help but look. Sure, Jake was drunk. But he was also right. That gator had been staring at them for the last half hour. As she watched, it sank below the surface, leaving only a ripple in the dark water.

Back in the cabin, Alex had transformed the wooden slat kitchen table into a buffet of fried catfish, cornbread, black-eyed peas, and…

"Is that fresh bread?" Simone asked, lifting the lid off the blue Dutch oven.

"Hell, yeah, it's fresh bread," Alex said, passing her a bread knife longer than his forearm.

Simone flipped the knife around and dug it into the bread, sawing off a huge slice.

"Dude, I am so glad you're a chef," Jake said. But before he could get another word out, he covered his mouth and ran for the front door.

Mia glanced at the door, then back to the table. "We'll save him the heel," she said. "Now pass me the bread."

Fifteen minutes later, Jake stumbled back in. From his pale complexion, food was likely the last thing on his mind. "Gator's gone," he mumbled before cracking open a new beer. He held it up. "Who's with me?"

Simone dashed over and grabbed a can. "God, I hope we don't run out." She turned to Mia. "You sure you brought enough for two nights?"

Mia had brought more than enough. Including the four cases they'd lugged into the cabin earlier today, she had three more cases tucked behind the seats in her Tundra out back.

"No worries if we run out," Mia said. "My great-grandma used to make moonshine in the shed out back during prohibition. All her shit's still there."

Simone's eyes went wide. "Show me."

Alex even stopped cleaning as they headed out the back door and toward one of the three smaller buildings.

Mia led them to the building on the left, about the size of a woodworking shed. The planks that made up the walls were aged to the point where the nails stuck out and the door hung by only one hinge. She pushed it open, making sure not to torque the hinge, then clicked on a flashlight.

The floor was rotting wood, with holes and dirt and weeds growing up through it. Against the far-right wall was a work table, covered in glass bottles so old they'd probably sell for hundreds on eBay. Some—okay, a lot—still had liquid in them, and about half of them were labeled, though the writing was so faded, it was hard to tell what they said.

Simone hurried over, oblivious to the rotting floorboards, and picked one up. "Who'll give me a hundred bucks to drink this?"

Alex dug in his pocket. "I got ten."

Simone pried the ancient lid from the bottle and sniffed it. She crinkled her nose. "Nope, ten's not enough…Well, not yet. Ask me after a few more beers."

"Hey, guys, check this out," Jake said from across the room.

Simone whipped around, setting the glass bottle back on the edge of the table. For two long seconds, it wobbled, until Mia dashed over and grabbed it, saving it from smashing everywhere.

"What'cha got?" Simone asked.

Alex pushed past her. "Is that a cookbook?"

Jake grinned. "A whole shelf of books."

Her parents had mentioned the shed when she was younger, but until they'd died, she'd never been allowed inside the moonshine shed. Her parents had always been overprotective. Now…they were gone, and she could do whatever she wanted. Still, it didn't make up for her parents' absence.

"Those must have been my great-grandma's books," Mia said, walking over to join them. "My mom always claimed her grandma was some kind of swamp witch."

"Like in Scooby Doo!" Jake said. "Wasn't that one of the episodes?"

"And we're the meddling kids," Alex said, grabbing a book off the shelf and flipping through a few pages. "No way. This is like some dessert mojo shit in here." He flipped a few more pages, then looked up at Mia. "Can I borrow this book?"

"You mean can you have it?" Simone asked.

"Forget dessert," Jake said. "Check out this book." He held out an aged brown book that looked like something forgotten in the basement of a used book store. Just barely visible on the cover were the words: *Brews of the Bayou.*

"No way!" Simone said. "Drinks!" She went to grab the book from Jake, but he pulled it away.

"Don't touch," he said, "or the spirits of the bayou are coming after you."

"You made that up," Alex said, glancing around the shed.

"Sure, but check this out." Jake opened to the first page. "The Crawdad Crawl: sure to give all who consume it the ability to scuttle like a crustacean. The Serpent's Sip: in which the recipient will turn cold-blooded for one hour, along with having a heightened sensitivity to vibrations. The Mudslide Mirage: Gives off the illusion of quicksand around whoever consumes the beverage, thus forming a protective barrier." He looked up. "I say we try the Crawdad Crawl."

Alex shook his head. "The Mudslide Mirage."

"To protect us from who?" Mia asked. Aside from the four of them and the gators, there was no one around for miles. Also, it was highly doubtful the gators would be fooled by some illusion.

Simone flipped forward a few more pages. "What about this one? The Gator Gulp: A cocktail guaranteed to bring the spirits of the swamp to life."

"Oh, hell yeah," Jake said. "And I'm finding that gator from earlier to feed it to."

"That gator is long gone," Mia said. Gone or hiding just under the surface of the swamp…waiting. She shuddered at the thought.

"That's what it wants you to think," Jake said.

Alex lifted the book from Jake's hands and carried it back over to the worktable. "What's the recipe call for? Let me read it."

The Gator Gulp

A brew to stir the swamp's soul and rouse its ancient heart—drink with care and beware—it awakens what lies beneath.

Ingredients:
- *2 oz Cypress-root bitters, freshly drawn for their strength.*
- *1 oz Swamp water, lightly strained to keep the bayou's essence.*
- *1 drop of Alligator blood—no more, lest the spirit grow restless.*
- *1 tsp Crushed Spanish moss, dried and ground fine.*
- *3 drops of Moonlit Dew, gathered under the waxing moon.*

> *• A splash of Crooked Stream water, to give the brew its twist.*

Instructions:
> *• In a bowl, mix the Cypress-root bitters and Swamp water.*
> *• Stir counterclockwise as you add the Alligator blood, drop by drop.*
> *• Whisper as you sprinkle the Spanish moss: "From root to scale, the bayou prevails."*
> *• Drip in the Moonlit dew, letting it shimmer as it touches the brew.*
> *• Finish with a splash of Crooked Stream water, stirring clockwise to seal its power.*

Serving Suggestion:

Pour into a wooden bowl and leave it open to the night air for a moment. Drink only if you dare bind yourself to the swamp's will.

Beware:

The Gator Gulp calls not only the spirit of the swamp but binds its power to the nearest vessel. Choose wisely where this brew is offered.

"I say we make it," Jake said. "I'm sure there's some way for us to get gator's blood."

"Even if we do, then what?" Simone asked.

"We get the gator drunk on it," Jake said, crossing his arms. "Revenge will be sweet."

Mia glanced around. All these glass jars and bottles. And these books. What had her great-grandma been up to here in this moonshine shed? Was it really moonshine or something way darker?

As her eyes scanned the shelves, the writings on the labels began to take form. Crushed Spanish Moss. Moonlit Dew. And…could it be?

"Hey, Jake?" Mia said, pointing. "I don't think you need to worry about getting the gator blood." She reached to a shelf and lifted a small glass jar about a quarter full of a thick dark liquid. As her fingers touched it, a chill ran through her, even though her back was slicked in sweat from the humidity in the air. "Looks like my great-grandma already got it."

Her great-grandma…the swamp witch.

Alex took that bottle from her hand, and then grabbed a few more. "Okay, help me carry these back to the cabin." He handed various bottles, along with a couple of ancient wooden bowls, to everyone. "If we're doing this, we're doing it right."

#   #   #

Ten minutes later, Alex stood in the kitchen over the wooden bowls. Four more beers had been opened, and the rest of the ingredients were gathered and organized on the counter. Simone reached for the Moonlit Dew.

Alex grabbed her hand. "Nobody touches anything except me. Got it?"

She scowled at him. "You need to chill out." She pushed herself right next to him and grabbed a wooden spoon. "I'm your sous chef. Now tell me what to do."

Seeing that there was no arguing with Simone, the two got to work, combining and mixing the ingredients. Mia tried not to watch at first, but as the bitters and swamp water got mixed, smoke rose from the wooden bowl, and she couldn't tear her eyes away. Was this the same thing her great-grandma used to do a hundred years ago? Had she really made alcohol during Prohibition or was that just a cover up for weird witchy swamp concoctions? She moved closer, leaving Jake lounging on the couch. As each ingredient got added, the air in the cabin thickened. The lights felt dimmer, as if the shadows were closing in around them. And when the last ingredient—the Crooked Stream Water—was blended into the brew, Mia held her breath, sure something was going to happen.

Three seconds went by. Then five. Thirty seconds and none of them dared say a word.

Then Jake said, "Let me smell it." He got off the couch and sauntered over to the kitchen counter, shoving his face into the bowl and taking a long inhale.

Alex shoved him out of the way. "You don't smell like that. You waft." Alex motioned with his hand, waving it over the bowl gently. "Didn't you ever take science?"

"Sure," Jake said, now wafting his hand. Then he went to stick a finger into the Gator Gulp.

"Stop," Mia said, grabbing his hand. There was nothing good that could come from him tasting the mixture. The warning at the bottom of the recipe tickled the edge of her mind.

The Gator Gulp calls not only the spirit of the swamp but binds its power to the nearest vessel. Choose wisely where this brew is offered.

"It's not for you," she said.

Jake yanked his hand away, then grabbed the bowl. "Fine. Now let's go find that gator."

The four walked out the door and onto the wooden front porch. For the cabin being so ancient, the whole place was in surprisingly good repair. Mia seemed to recall her parents saying they hired someone to patch the place up, maybe five years ago. Not that she could ask them now. She could never ask them anything again…ever. Had her parents intended to sell the place? And why had her mom never wanted her to hang out here?

"Now where's that gator?" Jake said. He scanned the water.

They all did. Mia looked out into the darkness. Stillness covered the surface—stillness and something deeper. More ancient. Spirits of the swamp.

No, that was ridiculous. Her great-grandma had probably lived out in this old cabin because everyone thought she was crazy—or because it was the best place to make liquor without getting caught.

"Wait," Simone said. "I think I—"

"I see it, too," Alex said, stepping up close behind Simone, pressing his back to her, like she was going to offer him some kind of protection. Actually, if it came down to it, Simone wasn't a bad option for protection. Sure, she wasn't about to wrestle off any gators with her bare hands, but the girl did have some martial arts skills.

Out in the water, in almost the exact same spot where it had been before, the alligator rose from under the surface. First its eyes, then its head. Its snout barely showed above the water.

"Are you sure that thing's real?" Alex said. "It reminds me of those gators they have on Jungle Cruise at Disney."

He had a point…except for one thing. This gator watched them. Its eyes were locked on theirs—on hers—almost like it was challenging them.

"Okay, I'm heading out to give the gator the brew," Jake said.

Even though Mia knew that was a horrible idea, she didn't do anything to stop him. There were so many things that could go wrong. He could fall in the water. He could trip on a root. He could get stuck in mud. He could get eaten by a gator—with or without barbeque sauce. But one step after another, and none of those things happened. Instead, he made his way toward the gator. All the while, the gator never moved. It watched Jake. It watched her.

When Jake was about fifteen feet away, that's about when his courage ran out. He placed the wooden bowl down on the muddy ground, turned, and ran back to the cabin. Once he dashed up the steps to safety, they all watched.

The alligator's gaze shifted to the bowl. Then it began moving forward until it reached the wooden bowl.

"What's it going to do? Lap it up like a dog?" Alex asked, barely in a whisper.

"Good question," Simone whispered back.

They didn't have to wait long to find out. The alligator opened its giant mouth, turned its head sideways, and consumed the entire bowl, Gator Gulp and all.

"No way!" Jake shouted. "I got an alligator drunk!" He put up his hand for a high five, which Simone returned.

But Mia was still watching the gator. With another tilt of its head, the bowl came back out, rolling and tumbling on the muddy ground. Then the alligator met their eyes once more. Except this time, instead of the fixed stare, its eyes were filled with unnerving intelligence.

"Does it look different to you guys?" Mia asked, blinking, trying to clear her vision.

"Maybe it wants some more," Jake said. "We can mix up more—"

"We're not making any more," Alex said.

"But do you guys not see that?" Mia asked. The stupid gator still watched them, calculating its next move. She took a step back. "I think we should go inside."

Jake put a hand on her shoulder. "You're imagining things. That gator's just drunk."

Okay, Jake did have a point. If the gator was drunk, it would be acting differently. But that didn't mean it all of a sudden became intelligent. What, was she going to give it an IQ test to find out?

Screw this. It was time for another drink—not some mixed up witchy concoction; a beer. This Bayou Brew stuff had gone far enough.

"Let's go inside," Mia said. She walked through the door, not glancing back.

#   #   #

That night, one and a half more cases of beer vanished. Mia dropped into bed—in a bedroom with two twin beds she was sharing with Simone—and immediately fell asleep. She woke to pitch blackness and a thick suffocating air that made her feel like she couldn't breathe. Mia sat up in bed, sucking in deep breaths, trying to fill her lungs. From the way she was gasping, she was sure she'd wake Simone, but there was only silence. And…no Simone. As her eyes adjusted to the darkness, it became clear that she was in the room alone.

"Simone?" she whispered.

At the sound of her voice, the silence from outside the window dissipated. The swamp came alive with chirps and growls and clicks, all familiar and yet intensified to the point where Mia would have slammed the window closed if it weren't so blasted stifling.

"Simone?" she whispered again, standing and moving to the window. The door to the room was closed, meaning whenever Simone did leave, she'd closed it behind her. As soon as Mia looked out the window, a shadow moved, tall and gliding across the muddy ground, toward the water. And then, the clicks and chirps of the swamp coalesced into a stream of words, ancient and unknown and filled with sinister echoes that wormed their way into Mia's mind.

Shit. She had to find Simone. Had to make sure everyone was okay. The last hour before collapsing into bed had been hazy at best.

Mia stumbled downstairs to find Simone sitting on the couch, rubbing her eyes.

"What are you doing down here?" Mia asked, then glanced to the open front door where Alex stood looking out. "Oh, I get it."

"Do you guys see it?" Alex said, not turning around to face them.

Chills ran up Mia's arms. "See what?"

"The shadows beyond the tree line," Alex said. "When I step forward, they move back. When I step back, they move forward."

Leaving Simone—who was still half asleep—on the couch, Mia tiptoed over to the front door, next to Alex. "Where?"

Alex pointed, his hand shaking slightly. "There." And pointing the other direction. "And there."

Mia strained her eyes but didn't see anything. "Show me."

Alex stepped forward, but as far as Mia could tell, nothing was moving. Whatever shadow she'd seen earlier was probably some animal, which was likely what Alex had seen also.

But when he stepped back, the ancient words filled her ears again.

"Do you hear that?" she asked.

"Only thing I hear is Jake snoring," Simone said. "They can probably hear him across the swamp."

That was true. Jake did snore, but why hadn't Mia heard him earlier? Regardless, at the mention, the disturbing grunts filtered down the stairs. Whatever Mia and Alex had seen or heard, none of it bothered Jake.

Alex stepped back from the door. "I don't see it now." He stretched. "And I'm beat. If I don't get some sleep, ain't nobody getting breakfast in the morning."

Mia stood at the doorway for another minute, listening and watching, but whatever she'd heard had stopped. The swamp at night was the swamp at night, and it was best handled with a closed—and locked—door.

#   #   #

Mia's stomach growled the moment she woke the next morning. She inhaled, hoping for the scent of bacon and eggs. Nothing. Alex must have still been asleep. And Simone was still not in the twin bed, meaning she'd spent the night downstairs with Alex. Mia had seen that coming for the last month, with their flirting escalating into something so sweet and tangible, it made Mia's head hurt. Or maybe that was just all the beer she drank last night. And had there been a bottle of whiskey? Mia threw on her sweat pants and gym shoes and headed downstairs. Three heads turned her way.

"What's everyone doing?" she asked, hitting the landing. And the better question was if Alex was awake, why wasn't he making breakfast? He lived for that.

Simone bit her lip. "Did you look out the window?"

"No, I just woke up," Mia said. She walked over to the window to the left of the front door. The curtains were wide open, and stifling air filtered through. How had her great-grandma managed to live in the swamp in Florida with no air conditioning? That sounded like some kind of torture.

"You see it?" Jake asked.

If this was about the gator again, Mia was going to make Jake sleep in the moonshine shed for the rest of the weekend. Then she looked out the window.

Staring back at her were a thousand pairs of eyes. Snakes, frogs, birds, deer, insects. There was even a panther. A freaking panther. All the animals stood unmoving, forming a perimeter in front of the cabin.

"What the hell is going on?" she asked, blinking to see if she was imagining the whole thing.

"They won't move," Simone said. "Alex tried yelling at them, but nothing happened."

Jake stepped up to join her. "I was thinking we should take a broom and try to shoo them away."

She whipped around to face him. "You're going to shoo a panther away with a broom?"

He shrugged. "Maybe?"

Mia blew out a deep breath. "If we go out on the porch, that should startle them. They'll all run away." Sure, that didn't answer the question as to why they were here in the first place, but it would get rid of the problem. It's not like they could stay cooped up in the cabin all day. They needed to get outside, get to the truck, get more beer, stuff like that.

"Good idea," Simone said, standing up from the couch. "I'll come with you."

As soon as Simone reached her, Mia wrapped her hand around the doorknob and opened the door. Warm air—no, air like an inferno—blasted into the cabin. And with it were carried the ancient words, filling Mia's mind. But that was a problem for later. First, to get rid of these animals.

She and Simone stepped out onto the porch. The animals didn't move. Their eyes stayed locked on the cabin, on Mia and Simone, unblinking. And despite the chirps and clicks they heard around the swamp, none of these creatures looked like they were making a sound.

Mia took another step, and something crunched under her gym shoe. She looked down to see the wooden bowl, complete and unbroken. Mia reached down to pick it up. Embedded in the bottom of it was a tooth—a single alligator tooth. Using her finger, she wiped the liquid that still clung to the bottom of the bowl. Lifting her finger to her nose, she sniffed it. It smelled like swamp water—except salty and sweet. That shouldn't be possible.

In that split second, the swamp came alive. The ancient words intensified, building to a crescendo. She still couldn't understand what they were saying, but their source became clear. The image of a giant creature formed in her mind, made of twisted vines and tree limbs and swamp water and bones. And even though she knew the creature couldn't be real, the sky darkened, and from the shadows, the creature emerged.

The horde of animals moved aside, making room for the hulking shadow, still hidden in the darkness. Clouds covered the sun. A stifling breeze picked up.

Next to Mia, Simone stepped back. "We need to get inside," Simone said.

Mia heard the words, but she couldn't tear her eyes away from the darkness. The creature's presence pressed on her.

"Mia, come on." Someone grabbed her from behind, pulling her back toward the door.

But her feet wouldn't move.

"Come on!" It was Jake, shouting.

Something about knowing Jake was freaked out managed to make its way into her brain. For Jake to be freaked out, the situation had to be real.

Mia dashed inside. Jake slammed the door after her.

A thump landed against the door, shaking the entire cabin. Simone let out a yelp and grabbed a walking stick leaning against the wall. She raised it up, like a bo staff.

"What the hell was that?" Alex spit out, stepping back, both from Simone and her stick and whatever was outside.

Another thump.

"Shut the window!" Mia shouted.

Jake rushed over to push the window down. A blast of hot air whooshed through, spraying water on his face before he finally slammed it shut.

All four of them edged backward until they were near the kitchen and the back door. Then there was silence.

"I feel it watching us," Alex said. "It's out there."

Mia could only nod. Whatever she'd seen, they'd all seen it. It hadn't been her imagination. It was real, and it was outside, in the swamp, with all the animals.

"Guys," Mia said. "Those animals…they weren't acting normal. What if—"

"What if it's controlling them?" Simone said, still clutching the stick.

"Not just the animals," Jake said. "Did you see the wind and water come through the window?" He reached up and wiped moisture off his face, bringing it to his mouth and tasting it. "It's swamp water. What if it…"

"Controls the swamp!" Alex finished. "It's the Gator Gulp. What did that recipe say?"

Jake ran into the kitchen and grabbed the Brews of the Bayou recipe book, flipping to the page where they'd found the Gator Gulp. "It says, 'A brew to stir the swamp's soul and rouse its ancient heart—drink with care and beware—it awakens what lies beneath,'" Jake read. "Shit, that's what we did. We brought the spirit of the swamp to life." He turned to Mia. "Your granny really was a swamp witch." Instead of sounding scared, his voice was filled with excitement.

"But those weren't real recipes," Mia said. "She made moonshine, not witch brews."

"So you think," Jake said. "But what if you're wrong? What if this is the real thing and we've brought this swamp spirit to life?"

His words hung there in the thick air of the cabin. There was no way. There was just no way. Except…the animals…the presence she'd felt. It couldn't all have been her imagination, could it?

Like her mind was trying to fool her, the darkness lifted, and sunlight again poured through the window. They waited, not moving, but the presence was gone. Mia dared to tiptoe forward and peek out the window. Aside from a couple of birds, there was no horde of animals looking back at her. Whatever had been out there was gone.

Simone lowered her stick. "Look, I don't care whether it's really real or not really real. We need to do something about it."

"Like what?" Alex asked. "Jake already got the alligator drunk. He's the one who did this. We can't undo that—unless anyone happens to have thirty pounds of activated charcoal."

Simone whipped around to face Alex. "Yeah, well, you're the one who mixed the recipe. Find a way to unmix it."

Jake, still holding the recipe book, grinned. "That's a great idea. Let's see what else there is in here." He popped a beer open, pulling on the tab until it broke off. After he shoved the tab into his pocket, he flipped the book back open, flopped onto the couch, and started reading. "Nope, not that one. Or that one. Or, oh, how about this one? The Offering of the Water's Will? It says *'To calm the waters and appease the Dweller, one must offer more than a brew—one must give their will.'"*

"Appease the Dweller," Mia said. "That sounds promising. What do we need?"

Jake rattled off a bunch of ingredients, including some of the same stuff they'd used before, along with a few new items.

"Bones of a Feathered Watcher?" Simone said. "What, do we have to slaughter a bird?"

"And alligator tears?" Alex said. "Do alligators even cry?"

"They do," Jake said. "I googled it. But it's not because they're sad. It's from pressure."

The way he said it, Mia could barely keep from rolling her eyes. What? Jake was some kind of alligator expert now when just last night he'd been trying to hit one with a beer can?

Mia held up a hand. "It doesn't matter why alligators cry. We just need the tears."

Alex pointed out back. "I say we check out the ingredients shed. See what your witchy granny has, and go from there."

Ten minutes later, either by harvesting from the nearby swamp vegetation or the Moonshine shed, they'd collected all but one ingredient.

"And we're back to Bones of a Feathered Watcher," Alex said. "What is that?"

"Maybe the book says," Jake said. He flipped to the back, and sure enough, there were a bunch of appendices. A few turns of the pages, and then he held it up. "Here. The Feathered Watcher."

A hand-drawn, colored-in illustration of a bird filled the page.

"What kind of bird is that?" Simone asked.

The bird was giant—like as big as a parrot on steroids—with mostly orange feathers except for black tips on the ends of its wings and tail.

"No idea." Mia pulled out her phone. "Let's Google Lens it." She angled in on the illustration, but nothing matched.

"You know, I swear this thing was one of those animals we saw earlier," Simone said. "I spotted it up in a tree."

"Which tree?" Jake asked.

So, book clutched in hand, they headed back to the house and onto the porch. Immediately, the swamp pressed in on Mia. But she did her best to ignore it.

"There," Simone said, pointing to a tree.

There was no sign up the Feathered Watcher bird, but there was—

"A nest," Mia said.

"Bet there are bones in that nest," Jake said.

"But look how high up it is," Mia said.

"And flimsy," Alex added.

Jake put up a hand. "I got this." With no delay, he dashed out into the swamp, the animal freak show from earlier absent. Once he reached the base of the tree, he jumped straight up, catching one of the lower branches. Then, with some swinging and pulling, he hoisted a leg over the tree branch.

Turning to face his friends, he gave a huge thumbs up.

"Please don't let this be the last of Jake that we ever see," Alex muttered.

Mia could only watch and nod.

One branch at a time, Jake climbed to the top, to the nest. Mia held her breath as he leaned over and peered into the nest.

"Babies!" he shouted down. "There are four babies. I think they think I'm their mommy."

The pressure coming from the swamp intensified, nearly causing Mia to drop to her knees. Whatever Jake was doing, the swamp didn't approve.

"Don't touch the babies," Mia called out, crossing her arms over her stomach.

Jake pulled back a hand that hovered over the nest. "But how do we get the bones?"

Mia twisted up her mouth as she thought. There was no way they could harm the mother or the babies. In no scenario that played out in her mind did that work out well. They all ended with Jake dead, likely falling from the tree after the mama bird clawed his eyes out.

"What else is in the nest?" Simone called up. "Take a picture and post it in the group chat."

Thirty seconds later, the image popped through on Mia's phone.

"Awww," Simone said. "They're so cute."

Alex held up his phone. "You guys see that—at the bottom of the next?"

Mia zoomed in on the image. Sure enough, covering the bottom of the nest, were the tiniest of bones. She went back through the words of the recipe in her mind. *Bones of the Feathered Watcher.*

And then her mind started parsing it down. Nothing said the bones had to actually come from the bird. As long as they belonged to the Feathered Watcher, which, in this case, being prey, they did.

"Jake, grab a few of the bones," Mia called out. "But don't touch the babies."

Jake nodded and reached back into the nest. At least he wasn't drunk yet…or was he?

She shook her head. Nothing to be done about that now. She held her breath.

Then Jake turned back to them, holding something up in his hand. "I got them!"

On cue the screech of a bird filled the air. Then it came into line of sight.

The Feathered Watcher. It was enormous, with a wing span that was as wide as Mia was tall. And with the way its eyes were narrowed in on Jake, it was pissed.

"Climb down now!" Simone shouted.

Jake cocked his head, as if hearing the bird but not seeing it. Then his eyes widened. He'd spotted it.

If there had been any alcohol in Jake's system, adrenaline forced it out as he scampered down the tree after shoving the bones into one of his pockets. But the bird was close. He wasn't going to make it.

Alex dashed into the kitchen then came back out with the bread knife in one hand and a diabolical look on his face. "Stand back," he shouted. "I got this!" He ran out into the swamp, shrieking and hollering, trying to distract the Feathered Watcher.

It worked. The giant bird shifted its sight from Jake to Alex. Jake wasted no time. He hurried back down the rest of the tree and ran for the cabin. Then he was inside…but Alex was still out there.

"Come on," Simone shouted at him. "Hurry!"

Whether it was her words of encouragement or the fact that the bird had nearly reached him, Alex sprinted like death was behind him—which it likely was. But the timing was perfect. Alex ran up the stairs, and once inside, Mia slammed the door.

From out the window, Mia spotted the bird. It rested on the railing. But instead of facing the cabin, it looked out into the swamp, where, once again, the animals congregated. Except this time, there were even more. And beyond the trees, where the swamp met the land, the alligator reappeared. Its eyes were locked on the cabin.

"Everyone into the kitchen," Alex said. "But turn out the lights."

Darkness filled the room. Then Simone picked up a lantern and lit it. "The eye of the swamp."

Then Alex spread out the ingredients on the kitchen counter and got to work. One ingredient after another, they all helped, taking hours. But as the last ingredient was added, nothing happened.

"Did you mess it up?" Jake asked. "Because I'm not climbing that tree again."

Alex shook his head. "We followed the recipe perfectly."

"Well, in that case, I say we give it a go," Jake said. He grabbed the bowl and headed back outside, out the front door. Mia, Simone, and Alex followed. The sun had long since set, and the swamp was filled with shadows.

Outside, the animals still watched, Mia's eyes glanced at the tree. Sure enough, the Feathered Watcher sat on a branch, protecting its nest, glaring at Jake as he stepped off the porch. He took a step forward, and the animals parted, creating a trail for him.

"Come on," Mia said. "We all need to go." She wasn't sure how she knew this, but she did. For the spell to be reversed, they all needed to be present.

Jake led the way, with Mia next, then Alex and Simone behind her. The animals turned to watch, closing in the gap behind them. There was no going back. This had to work.

As they neared the end of the path, darkness filled in every spot and crevice. But it wasn't just darkness from the fact that it was now close to midnight. Something waited for them. Mia felt it. And when it came into view, they all stopped walking.

"What is that?" Alex murmured under his breath.

"The Swamp Dweller," Mia said. "That's what we brought to life."

"Not brought to life," Simone said. "Revived."

She was right, this monstrous creature in front of them, half hidden in the mist, shifting with the darkness, was not something they had brought to life. It was ancient and powerful, made up of twisting vines and dark water. They had revived it, and now they needed to put it back to sleep.

Jake's hands shook as he stepped forward, still clutching the bowl. He placed it on the ground, in front of the Swamp Dweller, then scooted back.

As soon as he was with them again, the Swamp Dweller stepped forward, out of the shadows. The vines that covered it were alive, twisting around its body. Bones decorated its body, some so large they'd been snapped in half. And its eyes—they were eerie pits of murky swamp water yet filled with fire.

It bent down and sniffed at the bowl. But it didn't drink it. Instead, it raised back up and grinned, showing off wicked, brown teeth which had been filed into sharp points.

Ancient words filled Mia's mind. They seemed like nonsense, but then her mind began to parse them. Real words took their place.

"Sacrifice," she said.

"What?" Alex asked.

"Sacrifice," Mia repeated. "What's it say in the book?"

Simone, who'd been holding the book, flipped it open to the recipe for the Offering to the Water's Will. "There's this line," Simone said. *"To still the waters and soothe the Dweller, one must offer not just a brew, but their will."*

Alex twisted up his mouth in thought. "So, we got the brew right, but now how do we offer our will?"

The heaviness that had settled on Mia pressed with a new urgency. The animals had been silent as they'd started down the path, but now that silence vanished, replaced by chirps and growls and stomping. These animals would never let them leave the swamp, not so long as the Swamp Dweller was controlling them.

"Offer up our will…" Mia mused. She felt around in her pockets, then pulled out the alligator's tooth she'd found embedded in the bowl. She'd been planning on tying a cord around it and making it into a necklace. She held it up. "We all started this, and we all need to end this."

"Meaning what?" Jake said. "You think we each need an alligator's tooth?"

Mia shook her head. "We each need to offer a sacrifice. Give up something—give it up to the swamp." Without waiting, she stepped forward and placed the tooth into the liquid which filled the wooden bowl. The water bubbled and frothed and then settled back down.

"So, it doesn't have to be a tooth?" Simone said, running her tongue across her front teeth.

"Nope," Mia said. "But you each have to give up something."

Alex held up a small paring knife. "My uncle gave me this when I started in culinary school. I always keep it with me, kind of like a good luck charm."

He hesitated only a moment, then stepped forward and dropped the knife into the bowl. Again, it bubbled and frothed, this time with more flare.

Simone stepped forward next, holding out an earring. "My great-aunt gave me these. They're clip-ons, and vintage and…"

She let out a long sigh, then dropped the earring into the bowl. Again, it bubbled and frothed. There was also a slight color change, moving from murky green to orange—dull and flat, but orange nonetheless.

Three down. All eyes turned to Jake. He dug in his pocket, then held up a tab from a beer can—the same one he'd shoved in there earlier.

"Oh, come on, Jake," Mia said.

"Yeah, you need to do better than that," Alex added.

Jake shook his head. "You guys don't understand. I mean, sure, all you guys see here is a tab from the top of a beer can, but did you know that my uncle—well, my great-uncle—invented the pull-tab on top of soda cans? He came up with that shit. But it was never fair, because someone else claimed the invention as their own." He raised the beer can tab. "So, this tab here—it's so much more than just a beer can tab. This is history. This is my uncle never getting credit for what he invented. This is ingenuity in Midwest America back in the glory days when real people—not corporations—made a difference. When they had a chance for great success. This represents what America once was. What it will never be again."

Mia realized that she hadn't blinked the entire time he was talking. The words resonated inside her, of an America they'd always heard about but never lived in. Jake was right. This beer can tab was so much more.

Alex pointed to the wooden bowl. "Put it in."

Jake dropped the silver tab into the wooden bowl. There was a small bubble, then nothing. The Swamp Dweller who watched from the shadows must not have thought the offering was any good. Five seconds passed. Then ten. But when two more seconds passed, everything changed. The murky orange liquid flared to life, then transformed into a brilliant blue. Smoke and shadows crept off it. Bubbles rose and popped on the surface.

The Swamp Dweller stepped forward once more. This time, he didn't sniff the bowl. Instead, he picked it up, lifted it to his mouth, and drank deeply.

Mia held her breath the whole time. They all did. This had to work. They'd each given up something, and if that wasn't enough, they'd be in serious trouble.

For a second, it looked like the Swamp Dweller would fade away, back from wherever it came from. But then the ancient words filled Mia's mind once more. And what she heard…well, there was no way…

"What is it?" Simone asked, placing a hand on Mia's upper arm.

Mia shook her head. "It says it…"

"It what?"

Mia pressed her eyes closed, then let out a deep breath. "One of us has to stay behind. They need to be the Swamp Keeper. To ensure its rituals are respected. They need to bind themselves to the swamp for eternity."

Jake cocked his head. "Stay behind where? In the swamp?"

Mia nodded. "It's the only way to appease it. The only way for us to leave."

"You mean all of us except whoever stays behind," Alex said.

"That's what it said." Mia shook her head. Was this why her parents never let her visit her great-grandmother?

Jake crossed his arms over his chest. "I'll stay."

Nobody said a word. Mia had no idea what Simone and Alex were thinking, but her mind filled with a plan.

"No offense, Jake, but I'm not sure you're really Swamp Keeper material," Alex said. "It should be me. I'll stay. I was the one who mixed up the recipes after all."

"No!" Simone said to him. "You can't." But Simone didn't offer to stay herself.

Mia knew the next words she uttered could never be taken back. But this was the way things had to be.

"It has to be me," Mia said. "I have to be the Swamp Keeper."

All three of them argued with her, but nothing they said made a difference. It's almost like Mia had known this was coming since the moment she had stepped into the cabin after her parents' death. And as that thought worked its way through her brain, another one formed also.

"My great-grandma," Mia said. "She must have been the previous Swamp Keeper. That's why she lived out here—to always keep it at bay. But with her gone—and my parents gone—it's up to me to take her place."

No one said a word. Simone glanced to Mia, then to Alex, then Jake. The silence stretched on for an eternity.

Then Jake said, "So, you're going to be the next Swamp Witch?"

Mia nodded. "Yeah, I guess I am."

And even though they all tried a bit more to talk her out of it, it was half-hearted and lame and filled with resignation.

Mia stepped forward. The Swamp Dweller moved once more, out of the shadows, until it was only five feet from Mia. And though no words left her mouth, she conveyed her intention. When that was done, the Swamp Dweller receded into the shadows. Then animals around them drifted off back into the trees and swamp until they were out of view.

Mia turned around. "I think you guys should leave right away."

There wasn't a whole lot of convincing that needed to take place. Her friends dashed back inside to grab their stuff. In under five minutes, they were in the truck with the engine on.

"I'll come visit you," Simone said, giving Mia a hug.

"That sounds great," Mia replied, though she knew that would never happen.

As the truck pulled away, Mia watched. And once it was far out of sight, the realization hit her. She would never see her friends again. She would never leave the swamp. She would never…well, never do a lot of things anymore.

Well, there was nothing to do except to move forward, to make her plan. She, like her great-grandma before her, was now the guardian of the swamp. And if that was the case, then she'd better get started.

#   #   #

Simone sat up from bed, shaking herself from the dream. The nightmare. Since they'd left, she'd been plagued with horrible, vivid dreams every night. But this dream…it was different. She'd been back in the swamp, with the Swamp Dweller still there, hiding in the shadows. But when it opened its mouth to speak, Mia's voice was the one that filled her head. Worry filled her words, and dark shadows slipped around in the background. Then strange words flitted through Simone's head, and even though the words were in a language she didn't know, she understood them.

The Swamp Dweller would never be satisfied, not with just Mia. It wanted them all. And one way or another, it would get what it wanted.

\#   \#   \#

The Offering of the Water's Will
To calm the waters and appease the Dweller, one must offer more than a brew—one must give their will.

Ingredients:
- *Moss of the eldest cypress, gathered at sunrise, when the swamp lies still.*
- *Bones of a feathered watcher, fallen beneath the perch of an owl or heron—symbols of the swamp's ancient wisdom.*
- *Water from the Crooked Stream, drawn at dusk as the shadows lengthen and the current slows.*
- *Two drops of Alligator tears, to show humility and remorse.*
- *A sprig of swamp mint, to summon healing and balance.*

The Ritual
The steps are as sacred as the ingredients, for only through care and reverence may the Dweller be soothed.

Preparation
Find the place where the Gator Gulp was first offered—a clearing beneath the open sky, where the swamp's heart beats strongest. Build a small altar of cypress wood and place your ingredients before a single lantern, known as the "Eye of the Swamp," to draw the Dweller's gaze.

Mixing the Brew
- *Lay the moss into a clay bowl filled with Crooked Stream water, letting it steep.*
- *Grind the bones of the feathered watcher into fine dust and sprinkle them into the water as you murmur: "From the perch above to the depths below, the swamp is one, and one must show."*
- *Add the alligator tears, drop by drop, each paired with a soft confession of guilt for your disturbance.*
- *Lay the swamp mint gently atop the brew, leaving it untouched—a sign of respect.*

The Offering

Light the Eye of the Swamp and kneel before the altar. All participants must place a hand upon the clay bowl and chant together:

Water's will, we offer thee,
The swamp's soul, so wild and free.
Dwell no longer, release your hold,
And grant us mercy as foretold.

If the ritual is successful, the swamp will fall silent, and the Bayou Dweller will retreat into the depths. However, heed this final warning:

"The Will is never extinguished, only tempered. Those who break the balance again will face the wrath tenfold."

# # #

Author's note

Inspired by the bizarre headline *Florida man arrested for trying to get an alligator drunk*, *Brew of the Bayou* follows a group of friends whose spooky cocktail experiment takes a terrifying turn when they accidentally awaken an ancient swamp god. Now, with the bayou itself rising against them, they must race to appease the vengeful entity before it spreads its influence beyond the murky waters.

THE GHOST LAKE MERMAID

By Alethea Kontis

THEY CALL ME THE GHOST Lake Mermaid. Technically, the lake's named Cachichuma and I call myself Mer, though Jinna calls me Dahling, and the birds and fish have their own names for things. Every town like Buckle Springs has legends—Bigfoot, Chupacabra, Crossroads Demon, we've heard them all. (Jinna personally takes credit for the local resurgence of Bloody Mary.) Similarly, every lake has its own spirits. As far as I know, I'm the only mermaid. And that's fine with me.

My job here in Ghost Lake is to maintain the order of things. I stir the water so algae doesn't grow where the kids like to play. I encourage fish onto hooks, or discourage them, depending on the season. In the spring, I draw patterns in fallen petals at the water's edge. I even return lost things to the shoreline…unless they're shiny. I have a weakness for sparkles. Like the engagement ring someone threw off the Merry Death Bridge and the silver charm bracelet Jinna gave me with the symbols on it. She says they mean "truth" in Korean, but I don't know Korean, so I have to believe her. Believing Jinna's wild stories is part of what makes them so fun.

I also work to keep my own legend alive. An old ghost once told me that if my story faded, I would fade with it. I can't grant the wishes made on shiny coins tossed from the bridge, but I do catch them and keep them safe.

I've been known to flip a fin at anyone who cries into the water, to give them a bit of magic and maybe a little hope. And every so often there are children who, if they stare into the water long enough, notice my blue eyes looking back at them.

Sheriff Lee was one of those children. He's visited this bridge his whole life, stopping by after school, or while on Army leave, or during his daily run. Now he sips coffee and watches the sunrise, his thick black hair mostly gray. I know that one day these visits will stop. I'll miss him when they do.

"That man right there is my one regret."

Jinna always says this when Sheriff Lee comes to the lake. I hadn't noticed her beside me before she spoke, but once Jinna's present it's impossible not to notice her. Her lips are the same blood red shade as her voluminous evening gown and the string tied around her wrist, like there's something she forgot to remember. And she has this cloud of long, black hair that's silky enough to make a mermaid jealous.

But Jinna isn't a mermaid; she's a ghost. Jumped off the bridge a few decades back. On purpose. "I was magnificent," she told me. "If a lady has to leave a party, she should always do so while she's magnificent."

"The day he pulled my body out of this lake…mmm. We could have been sculpted by Michelangelo." Jinna fans her cheeks, as if we're surrounded by air instead of water. "In his prime, that man was a delicious specimen. Every woman in a hundred miles wanted to take a bite out of him."

"Why didn't you?" I ask even though I know the answer, because I love Jinna's stories.

"Child, he was maybe a dozen years younger than me, and from the only other Korean family in this one-horse town. We were probably related."

"You weren't related," I say.

"No, we weren't. But my dreams of ruining that divine man are surely far more exciting than the reality would have been." She sighs. "Surely."

I sigh with her for good measure. I like imagining happy endings for the ghosts of my acquaintance. I mean, if they'd actually had happy endings, they wouldn't have become ghosts to begin with.

"What are we looking at?"

I turn to the new voice. She's young, maybe half Jinna's age or less, making her presence all the more tragic. She's wearing jeans and a short leather jacket. A broken heart at the end of a faceted gold chain rests against her flawless brown skin. Her hair, made up of what seems to be a million tiny braids, floats around her head in a goddess-like halo.

Seriously. Another ghost with hair ten times more fabulous than my wavy golden tresses, and *I'm the mermaid.*

"The injustice of the universe," Jinna replies. "That's what we're looking at."

"Isn't an officer of the law literally the definition of justice?" The new ghost raises an eyebrow at Jinna's pointed glare. "I'm just sayin'."

"It's a long story," I tell her. I don't mention how many times she'll hear it.

"Well, you'll have to—oh my gosh, you're a mermaid!"

It's such a joy to make people (alive or dead) squeal in delight, as if their wild childhood imaginings have just been verified. Jinna didn't react at all when we first met, which I both loved and hated about her.

I wave cheerfully. "You can call me Mer."

She smiles back. "I'm Am…Amm…"

Brand new ghosts don't usually remember their names right away. They can maybe get out the first syllable. Same for the memory of their death. The more tragic the event, the tougher it is to retrieve. Some spirits don't realize they're ghosts at all. There's no use forcing it; the knowledge either comes with time, or it doesn't.

"We'll call you Amy for now," I say. "It's nice to meet you."

"I'm Jinna. How did you die?"

I roll my eyes. The question is just so…Jinna.

We watch Amy's face go through several emotions. First, she's surprised. Her gaze shifts from me to Jinna, and her brow furrows. Her eyes dart this way and that as she tries to remember something…and, wait… there it is. Her nostrils flare. Her voice comes back, deep and angry. "That man. *That man.* Bastard threw me off the bridge. Didn't even let me finish my sentence."

Almost unconsciously, her hand lifts to the broken heart at her throat. There's an R written there, not an A.

"Dahling." Jinna points. "Please tell me R isn't the one who killed you. You seem smarter than that."

Amy looks down at the necklace. "Renée is my girlfriend," she says wistfully. "The delusional asshole that was convinced I was into him was Joe…something. His number's in my back pocket."

The water will render that evidence worthless soon, if it isn't already.

"Don't worry," I say. "When they find you, they'll put him in prison where he belongs, and your soul can rest in peace."

"Or, you can haunt his ass so hard he regrets living," says Jinna. "Personally, I'd go with that one. Only…"

A look passes between Amy and Jinna. It's as if they're having an entire conversation in a language I don't understand.

"What?" I ask.

Jinna answers. "A Black woman gone missing in a town like this? The chances of anyone finding her…"

Amy shakes her head. "I'll be lucky if there's even a formal report."

"Oh. Right." Anger boils my blood. Just like legends, each town has its flaws, too. Ours is the Buckle family. Every last one of them is rotten to the core. Considering the quantity of tears wept into Ghost Lake over the last century, I know the depths to which the Buckles can sink. "Then how about we change this story?"

In a flash I'm off, swimming in large circles beneath the bridge, flipping my tail a few times so the sunrise on my turquoise scales catches Sheriff Lee's attention. Then I venture farther down, bit by bit, in ever-tightening circles until I find her at the bottom.

She is newly dead. Her dark brown eyes are fixed, wide and full of fear. They convey the scream that the duct tape over her mouth would have stopped. Her hands are bound with rope and chain, the skin of her fingertips already puckering. Her feet, bound in similar rope and chain, are tied to a cinder block. The broken heart necklace at her throat floats helplessly around her chin.

Poor Amy.

I look up—from this distance, the bridge is completely obscured by mud, algae, and a school of bream. I consider the placement of Amy's chains and the angle of the rising sun. If I time it right, it's possible the light might reflect enough for the chains to wink up at Sheriff Lee. If I can clear the way in time. And if he happens to be looking down at exactly that moment. And if he thinks that what he sees is more than just a fish.

It's a lot of ifs, but I'm determined to try.

I add my futile wish to the coins in the pouch at my side. Furiously sweeping my tail back and forth, I move swaths of algae toward the bank. When I spot red in the water I call to Jinna, "See what you can do about those chains."

Jinna can't move objects the way a mermaid can, but she's a mature enough ghost to be able to polish a few links of chain. She floats to the cinder block resting on the lake's bottom.

We both remember Amy's ghost too late.

"Don't look!" we shout, but Amy is already face to face with herself.

When ghosts meet the mortal flesh their spirit once inhabited, they typically either vanish or freak out. Amy surprises us both by opening her mouth and very calmly telling us a story.

I have only ever seen one ghost react this way. And once she'd started telling stories, she'd never stopped.

"I got too close. Investigative journalists live with that danger. But I was always two steps ahead, full of plans and exit strategies. Renée kept on me to work with a partner. She was right. Again. When brute force enters the chat, it's game over. Doesn't matter how clever you are."

The cool monotone of Amy's words gives me goosebumps, but I don't stop finning the water as I listen.

Jinna rises to the chains at Amy's wrists. "Who did this to you?"

"Joe"—it takes her a moment, but the name comes this time—"Buckle." Jinna snorts.

"Jinna!" I scold across the water.

"Dahling, please. What did she think was going to happen? The Buckles stole everything they ever owned, right down to the land that made up this town. To them, terrorizing anyone with skin darker than limestone is a sport. Amy-doll, you could have investigated until the cows came home. No charge is ever going to stick to that family. It never does." Jinna shakes her head.

"I'm sorry you wasted a perfectly good life for this."

Amy points skyward. "The sheriff is on my side!"

"The sheriff is an idiot. A beautiful idiot, I grant you, but an idiot just the same. If he had any sense, he would have left this town years ago. Just like I did."

Amy stares through Jinna. "If you left, then why are you here?"

"Because payback is hell." Jinna flips the hair already floating softly around her head. "I wanted every sad sack in this town to see my face in the headlines, above the fold. I wanted to haunt their children and their children's children for three generations, at least."

"Congratulations," Amy says flatly. "You won, I guess."

Jinna smirks. "Yeah, well…how far did you get?"

"Close enough to make somebody mad enough to kill," I point out.

Amy is not deterred. "Sheriff Lee said my best bet to nail the Buckles was if I found an old case, a cold case, one that could be solved using today's technology."

Right. The sheriff! I surface once more to check the bridge and see only blue sky and autumn leaves. Both he and his police cruiser are gone. Hopefully that's a good sign.

"No one talked, did they?" Jinna is saying when I sink back to the shadowed depth of Amy's corpse.

"Are you kidding?" Amy says. "I asked if Buckle Springs had any urban legends, and people couldn't *stop* talking. Folks love telling ghost stories, especially about their hometown. Didn't take me long to realize the answer had been staring me in the face the whole time."

"What was it?" I ask.

"The Merry Death Bridge," Amy says.

"Ooh," Jinna squeals. "The Dead Prom Queen Hitchhiker!"

"Wow. Yeah." I hadn't thought about that one in a while.

"How about I give Bloody Mary a break and haunt our merry bridge instead? Seduce strapping young drivers into taking me to the cemetery. Or just stand in the middle of the road and watch them drive straight into the lake." Jinna bats her eyelashes at me. "What do you think?"

I cross my arms. "Aren't you a little old to play prom queen?"

Jinna bends a wrist. "Dahling, don't get me started."

"That story is wrong anyway," Amy interjects before Jinna does get started. We both stare at her.

"Come again?" Jinna asks.

"The legend in Buckle Springs is that a teenage girl used her feminine wiles to lure some unsuspecting guy off the bridge to his death on prom night, right?"

"Right," I say.

Jinna grunts.

Amy's already shaking her head. "I spent ages digging for articles about that. What I unearthed instead was the record of a girl who went missing back on prom night in the 1940s. Her date wasn't the victim—he went on to live a long life. Had twelve kids and everything. But she was never heard from again. Their picture was in an old Buckle High yearbook. Her name was Meredith…something. She…"

"Oh, ha-ha," Jinna deadpans. "Meredith. 'Merry Death.' I get it."

"Is *that* why we call the bridge that?" It does make sense.

But Jinna is hungry for more of the grim story. "Then what?"

"She was…" Amy starts again, but the memories have vanished. She looks from me to her corpse and back again. Nothing else comes. I probably should have ushered us away from the body while we were talking. I admit, I'm surprised Amy's recalled as many details as she has. It's the mark of a powerful mind. She must have been crazy genius smart when she was alive.

Poor Amy.

"Sheriff Lee left," I say, changing the subject. "Hopefully, he saw the light."

"Or he just left," says Jinna.

I scowl at her. Can't she be a little sensitive to our newly dead companion?

"But our sheriff is still magnificent." Jinna raises her sharp chin. "If one must leave, one should always do so when they are magnificent."

This is a much better response. Amy asks the obvious question, which sets Jinna up to launch into the elaborate and distracting story of when, where, how, and why she made the very important choice to end her own life.

The "when" was a little over thirty years ago. The "where" was the Merry Death Bridge, of course. Jinna glosses over the gruesomeness of "how" and jumps straight into the far more romantic "why."

Simply put, Jinna had done everything. Graduated high school and left the embarrassing small town where she'd been born. Got a degree in mathematics in record time and left that, too, for a career on the stage. She'd had adventures (especially in Egypt), lovers (of every sort), and even a marriage (for five seconds). She'd built herself from the ground up, been swindled, cheated and/or robbed of everything she had, and then remade herself all over again. Apart from finding her One True Love or giving birth to a child, she'd checked pretty much every box life had to offer. And by the time she turned fifty, that last one wasn't an option anyway.

There she was: beautiful, successful, independent, bored, tired, and alone. So she returned to Buckle Springs (a.k.a. "the scene of the crime") and with her last breath, Jinna cursed this wretched little town and the family of bullies who founded it.

"But you led such an amazing life!" Amy says, at exactly the same point I always do. "What if—?"

"*What* if?" Jinna snaps. Because this is the question that ultimately sent her over the edge. Literally. The hopeful ones always ask this question.

"Fate had *fifty years* to track me down and cross my path with something or someone epic enough to make me care about living. I was tired of making my future up on my own, so I wrote my own ending. Nothing wrong with that."

"But—"

Jinna raises a finger. "You're stuck on the 'one true love' thing, aren't you?"

Amy nods and touches the broken heart at her throat.

"Me too," I whisper in solidarity.

"Dahlings." Jinna purses her bright red lips. "If there's a disappointed soulmate somewhere out there, then they'll just have to wait for my next life. Goodness knows they missed all the best parts of my last one."

"I have a love like that," Amy says to the broken heart.

"Then your love won't rest until she finds you," I say.

Amy nods, but I can tell she has doubts.

Jinna and I often reference the height of trees for telling time, or the colors of leaves, or the gray in Sheriff Lee's hair, but none of those have changed when a suited diver enters the lake beneath the bridge.

Much to my surprise, Amy's body is not rescued. Instead, the diver pulls out the black rectangle everyone uses for a phone these days, takes pictures from multiple angles, and then leaves.

"That's it?" I cry after the diver. Poor Amy. "You're just going to leave her here?"

"No, that's smart," says Amy. "My body needs to be removed from the water quickly, but carefully. You'd be surprised how much evidence they'll be able to get from that duct tape alone."

Jinna agrees. "Sheriff Lee learned the hard way what not to do when it comes to pulling a body out of this lake."

She means her body. He hadn't been an officer for very long then. The lake had been covered in cherry blossoms that morning. The world both above and below the water was eerily quiet. And then Jinna's spirit showed up and it was never quiet again.

Shortly after the diver's appearance, the water level of the lake starts to fall. It does that sometimes in the dead of the summer, when there isn't a lot of rain, but this seems more drastic. When I mention it to Jinna, all she does is look at Amy and say, "I guess the sheriff really was on her side."

Three divers on a flat-bottomed boat come next. The sheriff and a woman with curly hair the same amber as the autumn leaves watch from the bridge. She's small, but when she opens her mouth and screams, *"Amiya!"*, it shakes the trees. Sheriff Lee holds her back from climbing over the railing and jumping in herself.

Amiya, who is Amy no longer, holds a hand to her heart. "Renée," she whispers, and I can tell that her spirit is crying even though we're surrounded by water.

The broken heart at her throat turns to a flame that the lake does not extinguish. I've seen this spirit fire before, the angry swirling red, orange, and blue that consumes those who pass through the doorway to hell. But the broken heart flame does not consume Amiya. It merely sits at her throat, flickering.

Waiting.

When the divers cut Amiya's body away from the cinderblock, it falls back through the water and lands with a hollow thud, which is not the usual sound when large rocks fall to the bottom of the lake.

Eventually, Renée's screams fade away and the sky turns dark. The lake waters continue to recede.

"Why am I still here?" Amiya asks.

"It takes time for the living to find answers," I say. "Trust them. And trust yourself. I'm sure you were clever enough to make your murderer's identity crystal clear."

"And then?"

Jinna takes this one. "White light, peace, the whole shebang. Most souls jump through that doorway the minute it opens."

"Most souls," Amiya repeats.

"Judging by your bit of bling there"—Jinna draws a tiny circle in the water with her finger—"you'll get to choose."

"Choose peace," I advise.

"Or?"

Jinna grins. "Seek vengeance upon your killer. And his children. And his children's children. Three generations, at least."

"You don't want to do that, though," I say. "You are a smart, kind soul who deserves peace."

"And revenge."

"You're not helping."

"Aren't I?"

"Okay so what if," Amiya interrupts, "I choose vengeance, but only until the day Renée dies? Can I do that?"

I say nothing, because I honestly don't know. No spirit in this lake has ever done that before. Granted, no spirit in this lake has ever been offered the option before either.

Jinna is still grinning. "Yes."

I don't know if she says it because she knows somehow, or if she just really wants the Buckle family to be on the receiving end of Amiya's wrath for the next few decades. (Which I do agree they totally deserve.) Did the universe offer Jinna this kind of option after her body was rescued and she never mentioned it? The very idea of Jinna *not* telling a story like that is in itself fairly impossible to believe.

"They're going to stop draining the lake, though, right?" Amiya asks.

I've been wondering the same thing. The ghosts here don't need water to continue existing, but the fish are getting crowded. And I'm a mermaid. At this point, the water level is only a few feet above the cinder block. There's not a lot of room left.

I smile when I say, "I'm trying not to think about it."

The water's down to a foot above the cinder block when Amiya's white light appears. Sheriff Lee and Renée have found her justice at last. Amiya hesitates for the briefest of moments before reaching up to the swirling hellflame at her throat and making the choice I would never be brave enough to make.

"For love," she says, and the light grows and shifts, elongating into a sword of fire that ignites Amiya's dark irises. "And for all the victims of the Buckle family. I will make sure everyone gets what they deserve."

Jinna cheers as Amiya's spirit rises from the water up into the night, bright as a fallen star returning to the heavens. I should probably be worried about Amiya's soul being consumed by rage, but in this moment the only feeling I have is faith that the Buckles' luck is about to change.

And then the trucks come.

Sheriff Lee's cruiser pulls into his regular spot beside the bridge, but two larger vehicles with long arms and winches back as close as they can the water's edge, beeping steadily all the way. Wire ropes are unspooled to great lengths. Another boat with more divers appears on the bank.

Two burly men in waders enter the water and Jinna is interested. "What's this?"

I have never seen such an ordeal. "Something else to do with Amiya's murder?"

Jinna floats around the wading men's feet like a purring cat. "Or maybe something Amiya found."

The men pass their hooks to the divers, who disappear so deep into the algae that even I can't see them. It's as if they've burrowed beneath the lake itself. But they resurface, sans hooks, and give a shout. The trucks begin inching back up to the road.

And the cement block moves.

Because Amiya's body had not come to rest on the lake's bottom.

She'd landed on the roof of a car.

I can't seem to do anything but gape at the vehicle as it emerges, inching from the depths of the lake—my lake—into the sunlight. I know every inch of this water, I swear. Would have sworn. How did I have no clue that something this massive was sitting right under my fins this whole time?

But I do have a clue. Because I know that beneath that algae is a 1940 Hudson Convertible Coupe in harvest tan with sealed beam headlamps, two-tone upholstery, and automatic brakes that can stop on a dime even when the driver doesn't know the meaning of the word as he shoves his hand down the front of my dress. Mama spent every penny she'd saved on that stylish sheath covered in waves of turquoise sequins, form-fitting right down to where it flared out at the knee.

Brett Buckle, on the other hand, had worn a bad suit, half a bottle of whiskey, and a snarl when he realized how difficult it would be to yank up my hem. He chose to tear the dress off from the top for efficiency's sake. I fought back, kicking the gearshift and scuffing the dashboard. He hit me then, because how dare I mess up his daddy's precious baby. That's the last thing I remember.

Only it isn't.

I remember every ghost, every grievance that's drifted through these waters in the last eighty years. Every story. Every sadness. Every peace light and hellfire.

I know what happens next.

My revelation should feel like more than a fuzzy dream, but I've been a mermaid so much longer than I was ever alive. I have counseled countless torments. I have kept this town's bloody history as safe as wishing coins.

Sheriff Lee opens the passenger door.

Jinna's on the shore now, black hair and red dress floating about her as if she's still in the water. And for the first time since that car sank with a young girl still in it, I stand. Slow step by slow step I emerge from the lake on two bare feet, water beading upon turquoise sequins that are scales no longer.

"Don't look," Jinna whispers, but she doesn't mean it.

Not that I would've recognized the body anyway. There's barely a skeleton left, which is almost a shame. I would like to have seen that beautiful dress one last time. The dress I am still wearing. The dress Mama paid for with her blood, sweat, and tears.

I miss my mama.

Amiya comes back to the lake once more, the night Sheriff Lee finds my justice. "Brett Buckle's brother and three of his sons were on the police force," she reports, fire dancing in her eyes. "This murder wasn't the only thing they covered up. Sheriff Lee found so much evidence of corruption that almost every case handled in Buckle Springs is about to be overturned. He's handing files over to the state as we speak."

Jinna grins proudly. "Exactly the chaos this town deserves. I approve."

We stand at the edge of the low water like tourists. The lake will rise again one day, without me in it. Because swirling in the air now are two bright lights: peace and hellfire. It seems the universe's offer to Amiya wasn't as rare as I thought.

"Which will you choose?" Amiya asks.

Jinna immediately opens her blood red lips and I know what she's going to say, but what comes out is, "Choose peace."

I know this. I feel it from the ends of my wavy golden locks to the tip of what is no longer my tail. I know she is right and that it's well past my time, but…

My eyes must convey what my mouth doesn't.

Jinna laughs, deep and throaty. "I've watched you patiently shepherd every soul that's passed through this lake for the last thirty years. If anyone deserves to rest, Dahling, it's you."

No longer trusting my voice, I point to the turbulent hellfire.

Amiya closes her hand gently over my own. "I've got the vengeance covered."

"And I will make a magnificent mermaid."

I resist rolling my eyes at Jinna. Heaven only knows what sort of guidance she'll pass along to the next generation of dearly departed. With luck, there won't be too many.

But I have hope. Because her current advice is exactly what I would have said to some poor unfortunate soul, had I still been Ghost Lake's Mermaid.

"Thanks for making this easy," I tell them.

"Thank *you*," they both say in return.

But there's one more face I want to see before I take that last step into oblivion. He arrives at dawn, like he has almost every day since he was a boy, and parks his cruiser in the usual spot. Instead of walking onto the bridge, he shuffles down to the edge of the low water. Gold and amber leaves fall upon his hair and uniform. His boots leave footprints in the mud.

"Thank you, Sheriff Lee," I say, even though I know he can't hear me.

The rising sunlight winks upon the small pile of shiny treasures I've left for him, including an engagement ring and a sack of coins. He crouches down and picks up a bracelet with silver charms. There is a red string tied around his wrist, as if to remind him of something he will never forget. A fin breaks the water before us. We both know who it is. I'm going to miss her, too, the best friend I never had in my last life. I hope our paths do cross again in the next.

In the meantime, if a black-haired ghost in a fancy red ballgown stares you down from the middle of the road on the Merry Death Bridge, be sure to say hi for me.

CARETAKERS

By Will McDermott

To: Agent F. Mulder, FBI Headquarters, Washington, D.C.
FROM: Ms. Alex Betts, Roseville, California

Dear Agent Mulder,

First off, I need you to know that I am not crazy. I do know you are a fictional character from an ancient television show and that there is no X-Files division at the FBI.

That being said, I certainly hope there is someone there who actually investigates weird, paranormal cases. I mean, someone put together that report on UFOs a few years back!

So, I'm hoping that addressing this package to you will get it into the hands of the real-life agents assigned to the real-life X-Files division. You understand, don't you? I need you to be real because the shit I am about to tell you is very real.

You may not recognize my name, but I was briefly famous last year when I rescued a lost cat that had somehow traveled all the way from Yellowstone National Park in Wyoming to my town of Roseville, California. That's 800 miles! Amazing, right?

Maybe I should have suspected something was strange about that cat at the time, but it seemed so normal, and it was half-dead, so I just wanted to protect it. But that's exactly what it wanted me to think.

I'm getting ahead of myself. Let me tell you how I found the tiny booklet included with this letter and then you can decide for yourself if something about all of this is weird. When you read it, you'll know I'm not crazy.

After I took Rayne Beau… That's the cat's human-given name; you'll see he calls himself by another name. After the Placir SPCA reunited Rayne Beau with the Anguianos family in Salinas, I went back to the green space across from my office where I originally found him. I heard he had lost his collar and hoped to be able to return it to Benny and Susanne Anguianos.

Well, I found the collar inside the same culvert Rayne Beau had crawled out of. It was covered in blood. But that wasn't the weird part. Hanging from the collar was a bulging pendant with a bent hinge. I forced it open, thinking there would be photos of the Anguianos couple and Rayne Beau inside.

But when it popped open, I found the tiniest little booklet I've ever seen. The whole thing was bulging from being wet, so I had to dry it out completely before looking inside.

I wish I'd never opened that booklet. I wish I hadn't read it. In fact, I wish I had left the whole thing alone. My life would be so much better right now if I had never gone into that roadside ditch green space in the first place when I heard Rayne Beau—that so-called cat—mewing.

I don't know what to do now. I can't sleep. I'm scared for my life. I'm scared for the lives of the Anguianos family. So, I've sent the booklet to you. Read it and you'll know I'm not crazy. Maybe you can do something about what happens next. I'm washing my hands of the whole thing. I need to regain control over my life. I may even move.

Yours in fear,
Alex Betts

#   #   #

Mission Log — June 5, 2024

Caretaker Akicitas reporting. I am on my way to the place the New

Humans call Yellowstone—what the Ancient Tribes called the Burning Mountains. The tribes knew better than to travel through those scalding, hot lands. They knew the dangers. Modern humans never believe anything can harm them. That's why we Caretakers must stay vigilant.

I would have started earlier, but my current host family have been somewhat difficult to train. After I got the call about the situation with Caretaker Akiassee, it took some time to convince Benny and Susanne they needed to go on a thousand-mile camping trip.

We should arrive tomorrow and then I will begin my hunt. I hope Akiassee fully recovers. We've worked together several times, including when we quelled the Old One uprising that caused so much damage around the Great Western Bay a century back.

Mission Log — June 7, 2024

We entered the Burning Mountains today. After giving Susanne the slip, I made my way toward the spot where Akiassee was ambushed and picked up the scent of my prey. But something was off. It was definitely wendigo. Their stench is unmistakable. But there seemed to be a lot of them. I could barely breathe from the overpowering acrid taste in the back of my mouth and nose.

Perhaps an entire family had been turned, but in all my years, I'd never seen more than two wendigo banded together. Of course, I'd heard the tales of what happened in the area the New Humans call Donner Pass, but I don't know how that disaster could happen today. Still, my nose doesn't lie. There were at least a half-dozen monsters, maybe more.

Plus, there was something else. I caught just a whiff of a different scent that was almost completely masked by the foul odor of decay and rotting flesh. Something much older. I'm not certain what. But if I'm right—if something more dangerous is working with the wendigo—it might explain how a warrior of Akiassee's stature could have been ambushed.

I followed the pungent trail to an abandoned ranger cabin deep in the woods. I knew Susanne would worry if I didn't return before morning, but she would wait for me. I trained her and Benny that well, at least.

Besides, something about the cabin was gnawing at my hind leg as well. I wasn't sure what it was, but I dared not leave until I figured out the double mystery of the cabin and the odd odor. So, I decided to stake out the cabin to see what transpired. The last thing I wanted was to make the same mistake as Akiassee and rush in without all the information.

Mission Log, June 10, 2024

Scat! My impatience nearly cost me a life today. I fared better than Akiassee, but the mission is far from over. Here's what happened.

The wendigo family returned to the cabin late last night with their latest kill—some poor hiker who must have wandered too far off the trails. The hiker was already half-eaten when they returned, so I decided to watch for the extra scent to show up and also wait for the wendigo to sleep off their feast.

A couple hours before sunrise, no other monsters had appeared. I didn't want to risk any early risers, so I slipped into the cabin through a broken window and padded over to the closest wendigo.

It's leathery skin was drawn so tightly against its ribs, hips, and limbs that it looked almost skeletal. Wendigo eat and eat and eat but remain ravenous. That's what makes them so dangerous. But that was about to change.

I extended my claws and raked them swift and hard across the exposed neck of the closest monster. It barely gurgled as its last breath escaped through the long slits in its throat.

One down, six to go.

I made my way methodically around the cabin, slicing and dicing wendigo throats into shredded ribbons of meat, cartilage, and bone.

I had just two left, but when I reached the penultimate wendigo, that other scent, something foul and ancient, wafted off the corpse-like body. I admit it. I hesitated. And that almost cost me a life.

Before I could rake my claws through this monster's neck, it's eyes fluttered open. Big, yellow, canine eyes! It was a scatting skin-walker wearing the skin of a wendigo.

My claws slashed down toward its exposed neck, but the skin-walker was too fast. It grabbed me by the collar and flung me across the room before jumping to its feet.

I landed on my feet, of course, and prepared to leap back into the fray. I couldn't kill it without learning its true name, but I could make it wish it were dead—for Akiassee's sake—while containing it until reinforcements arrived.

But the skin-walker was smarter than I gave him credit for. I realized my paws were ice-cold. I had landed on the chest of the last wendigo. Their cannibalistic hearts truly are made of ice. Its chest was actually frosted over, forcing me to extend my claws to leap back into the fray. But, when the razor-like tips dug into the monster's leathery skin, it awoke with a roar.

I tried to pounce back at the skin-walker, but the wendigo lashed out as I leapt and sent me sprawling across the floor. Before I could turn around, the ice-hearted monster was on me again. They move fast for starving, half-frozen cannibals.

I had precious little time to deal with the last wendigo. If the skin-walker caught me again, it would be nothing for it to rip me in twain in its powerful, wolf jowls. Which I'm sure is what happened to Akiassee.

So, I dashed up the wendigo's bony legs and sliced my claws right through its groin, twice, back and forth. This made the beast double over around me, protecting me for the moment from the skin-walker and bringing its fleshy neck into range of my claws.

With one more slice, the last wendigo crumpled to the dusty floor, as dead as its brothers and sisters. But, for the moment, I lay trapped beneath it, caught in the leathery folds of its limbs and torso.

By the time I clawed my way out to freedom, the skin-walker had disappeared.

Mission Report, June 13, 2024

I tracked the skin-walker back to the campground where I had left Benny and Susanne. For a moment, I feared for their lives, although the skin-walker had no reason to target them specifically. Luckily, they were up early and away from the camper. Apparently, they were off searching for me. I could hear Benny rustling through the woods calling my name.

I wanted to go to them. Let them know I was okay. They're good humans, and I didn't want them to suffer because of me. But that's exactly why I needed to stay on the trail of the walker. He would kill again, and once he did, he would take a new skin, and I might lose him.

I couldn't let that happen.

I turned away from Benny's calls and prowled through the campground, following the beast's pungent odor. I didn't find the walker, but the scent lead me to his wendigo skin, abandoned in the bushes near the showers, next to the skinless remains of a woman who's only mistake this morning had been wanting a shower while the skin-walker sought a new skin.

I felt like I'd coughed up a furball. My mistakes had cost some poor human their life.

I moved away from the acrid smell of the dead wendigo skin and skinless dead human to search for the skin-walker scent again. It took me a while, but I finally found the scent, which had been heavily masked by soapy shower water and less-soapy bathroom fumes.

Why humans are willing to bathe where they defecate is beyond me, but at least I had the trail again, which led toward the campers at the far end of the camp. As I began padding in that direction, I heard a camper engine roar to life.

I reached the edge of the campground in time to see a Winnebago tear around the edge of the lot toward the exit. The driver, a woman who's skin looked ill-fitting glared back at me. Her yellow eyes shone briefly in the fluorescent lights at the edge of the access road.

I tore through the forest toward the main road to get ahead of the big, slow camper. I had to see which way it turned. I got there just in time to see it head southwest. Not much to go on, but I had to try.

I looped back to the campground. Benny and Susanne were deep in the forest searching for me, so that was going to take too long. Luckily, I saw a family packing up. I hopped in the back of their SUV and began meowing like my life was in peril. Which was only half a lie.

It felt like I spent an interminable amount of time convincing these people to both hurry up and to take me with them. But in reality, it probably took less than fifteen minutes. They had obviously been very well trained by a previous cat-master.

Soon, we were tooling down the highway, heading west. I convinced them to open the window so I could track the skin-walker. Any other beast I would have lost, but it's strong scent carried on the wind for miles, which was lucky because it turned onto a highway heading almost due south within just a few miles.

At least we were heading in the right direction. Every time this nice family tried to turn away from the skin-walker's scent, I caterwauled loud and long until they changed their minds.

I'm sure they thought they were returning me to my home. Little did I know that this ruse would become too true for me all too soon.

Mission Log, June 18, 2024

After days of forcing my temporary family to drive almost due south through Wyoming and Utah, we entered Nevada and began heading west again. Then, yesterday morning, I forced them to turn into the parking lot of the Overland Hotel and Saloon in Pioche, Nevada, where the skin-walker's trail ended.

I don't know why the skin-walker brought its new family here. Perhaps it just needed a rest or had figured out I was on its trail and wanted to change bodies and cars again. But it seemed like a gigantic coincidence that it chose this hotel of all places. You see, I have some history here.

The current Caretakers Council members may not remember, but I was sent here more than 200 years ago to handle a "ghost" problem. Just like this little "wendigo" job, the Overland Hotel ghost turned out to be anything but a ghost. I had to employ an actual catholic priest to exorcise that damned demon.

But I digress.

Whatever the reason, the skin-walker had brought me back to the Overland. It turned out it even booked Room 10, the very spot where the exorcism took place. But, again, it all could be a coincidence. The hotel went to great lengths to play up the "Ghost Story" of Room 10. It was in all the brochures. Of course, they got every fact wrong and didn't even mention me.

But he was here, and I needed to stop him before he killed again. So, as soon as we stopped, I leapt through the open window of the SUV and ran straight into the hotel lobby and began cuddling up against the desk manager, a young woman by the name of Adele who, coincidentally, was the great-great-granddaughter of the woman who ran the place back when I saved the day, no thanks from any of the humans, as usual.

When my temporary family rushed in and found me seemingly at home, they asked the manager if I was her cat. I cuddled hard against her face and mouth before she could answer. She shrugged at them and said, "Sure looks like it."

And that was that. I had freed my transportation to get on with their lives. I hoped they decided to head back out immediately, but they decided to stay the night.

I needed to get that skin-walker before he got to them.

Late last night, I slipped into Room 10 to deal with the walker once and for all. The room looked almost identical to how it had 200 years earlier, except with a lot less blood on the walls. The stench of the beast I was after filled the room and my nostrils.

It was everywhere.

I checked the two cots before moving to the main bed. Each had a young child fast asleep, but reeking of skin-walker. I began to get a very bad feeling about this situation. I made my way to the four-poster bed. Atop the thick mattress lay the father, who also reeked of skin-walker.

But none of them had been replaced. The monster had simply covered them in its pheromones to throw me off. The mother of the family, the woman who's bloody carcass I had found near the wendigo skin in Yellowstone, was nowhere to be seen.

I dashed from the room and down the hall to the room where my temporary family were sleeping. But there was no walker stench emanating from that room. I slipped inside just to be sure, and I could see them all asleep by the light of the nearly full moon streaming through the window.

The full moon. Like werewolves, the skin-walkers' distant, European cousins, these new world shapeshifters drew power from the moon and were never more dangerous than under the influence of the light of a full moon. And it's not just the one day, either. Most books get that wrong. Shape-shifter attacks peak on the day of the full moon, but the two days leading up to it and after it are just as dangerous.

I had to find the walker fast. But where had it gone? If it was still intent on evading me, I thought it might grab the skin of a horse. It had been a wendigo, so why not another mindless beast? That would give it speed and the ability to avoid roads, which would slow me down.

I jumped onto the windowsill to look down on the stables behind the hotel. Sure enough, I saw the yellow-eyed woman sneaking toward the barn doors. But I also saw a light on inside the stable! Someone was in there, and I was fairly certain I knew who.

I jumped from the window and landed on my feet on the ground fifteen feet below. I raced toward the stable but heard the screams as I crossed the distance.

The stable doors were slightly ajar, so I ran for the crack between them. I planned to rush in and confront the shapeshifter as it worked to don its victim's skin.

But I underestimated the speed the moon's power gave it. Before I reached the doors, they slammed open and great-great-granddaughter Adele, eyes flashing yellow, rode through the widening doors atop a great stallion. She disappeared into the night, once again heading west.

Mission Log, June 21, 2024

After losing the skin-walker in Pioche, I hopped a train to Carson City. I had a pretty good idea where the beast in granddaughter's clothing was going next, so I wanted to get ahead of him for once.

I'm not sure why, but this skin-walker seems to have a grudge against me. I finally figured it out when I realized why that abandoned cabin in Yellowstone made my hind leg itch. Caretaker Akiassee and I had worked another case together that led to that very cabin. So, the Akiassee attack and use of the abandoned ranger cabin where the two of us had banished a swarm of mosquito men was just to lure me out.

Then, the next place the walker stopped was the Overland Hotel. And of all the people he could choose for a new skin, he just happened to grab the great-great-granddaughter of one of my former human pets.

The bastard was targeting all my greatest wins and trying to turn them into losses. I didn't know why, but it didn't matter because I had him. The walker was headed for the Clown Hotel in Tonopah, Nevada. I won't describe what happened there. If you want to know, look up the sanitized version in the annals. That place still haunts me and I won't discuss it.

But I wasn't going to Tonopah. At least not yet. First, I had to visit an old friend in Carson City. I didn't know this skin-walker's true name, so I needed a medicine man who could create a sacred weapon.

Luckily, I knew a guy. Well, the grandson of a guy, but he went into the family business.

As soon as I walked into Setting Son's shop, I could feel the power of the place. The kid, now pushing 80 himself, looked up at me and flashed a huge, wide grin that nearly cracked his ancient, brown skin.

Turns out, Son had been waiting for me. He'd heard about the strange happenings across Wyoming and Nevada and just knew I had to be in the middle of it all.

I leapt onto the counter and sidled up against Son. I'd forgotten how much I missed a little human contact. I told him I was tracking a skin-walker who seemed to know a lot about me, so I needed an edge—the edge of a sacred weapon to be exact.

He had just the thing.

Son reached beneath the counter and pulled out a short, curved blade with a leather-wrapped, bone handle. Red and black ribbons trailed from the guard, representing power and death respectively. The ribbons had been tied on with what I could tell was cord made from the intestines of a bison for a little extra oomph.

I didn't ask where he'd gotten that particular, very illegal, ingredient as he handed me the blade. Good thing, too. Son had more than just the blade for me. He had intel on the skin-walker I'd been trailing.

Son told me the walker had already blown through Tonopah two days earlier, where he'd taken the current owner of the Clown Hotel, before heading toward Carson City. Once in Carson city, the walker didn't waste any time in his clown skin.

He apparently grabbed some kid right out from under the noses of her parents while they toured Bliss Mansion during a "Ghost Walk."

That tracked. I worked the Bliss Mansion haunting way back in the

Wild West days. Scatting railroad baron built his house atop an actual tribal burial site. Son's grampa and I had to put all those poor souls to rest before they took out the whole town.

I asked Son where I could find this kid as I twirled the sacred blade between my claws. After admonishing me about talking about a kid like that while twirling a blade, Son gave me the bad news.

The walker's new family had already left Carson City on their way to Reno. But he said that after Reno, the parents were heading to Roseville, California.

That tracked. I had business in Roseville a couple decades ago. Nothing in Reno, though, so maybe that side trip wasn't part of the skin-walker's revenge plot.

Better yet, Son had arranged quick transportation for me to Roseville. Now, Setting Son knows I hate planes, especially small ones with open seating, so I was not at all surprised to find that his "quick transport" was a single-engine crop duster owned by a friend of his.

But to his credit, Son gave me one last bit of information he'd discovered about the skin-walker before I took off for Roseville. Apparently, I knew this walker's sire. In fact, Akiassee and I had killed his sire about 50 years ago. Son didn't know the walker's name, though, but now that I had the sacred weapon, I didn't need the bastard's name.

Mission Log, June 24, 2024

Well, everything went according to plan… until it didn't.

The address Son had given me for the family whose daughter the walker had replaced was accurate and I arrived before they got home from Reno.

Several hours after the lights went out inside, I slipped through an open window and followed the ancient stench of the skin-walker straight to the girl's room. I even checked the parents' room first to make sure the scatting walker didn't fool me again by spreading his scent around the family.

Everyone was asleep, so I padded back to the girl's room, where the stench was the strongest. She lay there asleep in the dark, reeking of decaying skin. I had him. Finally. It seemed certain I would finish this hunt right then and there.

I padded into the girl's room, leapt silently onto the foot of her bed, and prowled up toward her head—and her exposed neck, the sacred blade clenched between my teeth.

I grabbed the blade from my mouth, raised it over her slender neck, and mewed the proper prayers to summon the sacred spirits to aid me in dispatching this abomination of evil.

That's when the lights flared to life overhead, the mother shrieked behind me, and everything went to scat.

The walker's yellow eyes, too big for the little girl's cherubic face, flashed open beneath my blade as I tried to plunge the tip into the tender flesh of his throat.

The mother shrieked again and rushed forward. The walker raised its spindly, child arms to fend me off, but only managed to divert the blade to the side. It bit flesh but missed the carotid.

The mother slammed into me before I could pull the blade free to try again, sending us both tumbling off the bed. I landed atop her chest and pounced back up onto the bed, hoping to finish the job before anything else went wrong. The mother might send me off to a shelter afterward, where I would be put down for killing her baby, but at least the job would be done.

Except, of course, I no longer had the blade. He did.

As soon as I landed on the bed, I saw the blade flash toward me. The walker had no strength in those spindly, little-girl arms, but he still had the speed and experience of a monster to guide it home.

The sacred blade plunged into my abdomen as I tried to twist and leap out of the way. Blood streamed from the wound and matted my fur. The walker raised the blade again, the blood spilling from his own neck wound running down his slim arms to wet the blade.

Behind me the mother had risen and screamed bloody murder at me. Caught between protective parent and knife-wielding child monster, I had no choice but to flee. I leapt at the mother's face, forcing her to duck and raced through the house for the open window where I had entered.

Mission Log, July 29, 2024
It's been a month since the bedroom debacle. I haven't had the time

or strength to complete a report in that time. Since the walker stabbed me, I've been on the run. I patched the wound the best I could, but I lost a lot of blood—and that was before the wound got infected.

On top of that, the walker has been hunting me. First it came for me in the body of the mother. I'm sure she was taken soon after she witnessed her own daughter nearly fatally stabbing a demon cat. Poor woman. She didn't ask for that. None of them did.

I don't care a hairball for my life at this point. I failed the humans of Roseville and everyone between here and Yellowstone. He's taken so many in the relentless pursuit of his petty revenge. I should just let him take me and be done with it. But I know the killing won't stop there.

I need to find some way to get this report to the Council, so they can send another Caretaker to finish the job I failed. But I can feel him closing in. Even if there were another Caretaker in Roseville, I couldn't get my logbook to them before he catches up to me.

I need help. I'm sure he'll find me here in this drainpipe any day now…

#   #   #

Ring-ring. Ring-ring.

"Hello?"

"Is this Ms. Betts? Ms. Alex Betts?"

"Who's calling?"

"You can call me Mulder. Agent in Charge Mulder. I'm with the FBI Extraordinary Cases Unit. And no, that is not my real name, but I think you know why I am calling."

"You got my package."

"Yes, ma'am. I have agents on their way right now to the Anguianos residence in Salinas, but I have a few questions."

"I was sure you all were going to think I was crazy."

[Silence]

"Yes, ma'am. We get that a lot. Can you tell me where the rest of the booklet is? The reports you sent us were incomplete."

"That was all I found. That's why I was so concerned. As far as I know,

Rayne Beau, or Akicitas as he calls himself, never made another mission log. I think that creature must have found him and killed him. I think the skin-walker took Rayne Beau's skin and tricked me into returning him to the Anguianos's home so he could complete his revenge."

"Not possible, ma'am. Rayne Beau was identified by his microchip, which is placed subdermally, meaning it's implanted beneath the skin."

"I know what it means! But what about all that blood on his collar? Where did that come from?"

[Silence]

"Hello? Agent Mulder? Hello?"

#   #   #

"Just a routine check-in, right?" Agent Hayes asked as they exited the sedan. The sun was shining, and the street was calm and almost too suburban for Hayes's liking. It was the place white people went to die long, lonely deaths. He'd never be caught dead living here.

"Yeah," replied Special Agent Matthews. The AIC thinks there's nothing here. We just need to follow up to be certain."

As they walked toward the front door, Matthews hesitated beside Hayes and then reached into his inside jacket pocket to grab his phone, which was buzzing.

"Speak of the AIC," he said, waving the phone in the air. "Go ring the doorbell while I see what he wants."

Hayes gave his senior partner a quick thumbs-up, but he already knew what their boss wanted. The man had only recently been promoted and had not yet learned the fine art of managing without micromanaging.

Hayes didn't give the matter another thought as he rapped his brown knuckles on the red door set into the white front porch. *What was it with white people and their red doors?* He wondered as he heard an old person shuffling toward the door inside. *Not enough color in their lives?*

The door opened and Hayes nodded at the short, plump Mrs. Anguianos. Almost white, gray hair surrounded her face in a style she'd probably worn since watching *Friends* in college.

"Mrs. Anguianos?" Hayes inquired. "I'm Agent Hayes with the FBI. May I and my partner come in for a few minutes?"

Hayes motioned back to Matthews, who seemed a bit animated for someone just providing a check-in to an overbearing boss.

"What is this about?" Mrs. Anguianos asked. "We're not in some sort of trouble, are we?"

She glanced over her shoulder and cried out, "Benny! The FBI is here. Did you and your drinking buddies break that pinball machine again?"

"Hayes!" Matthews yelled behind him. "Hayes! Step away from the door. Right now!"

Hayes glanced back at his partner, who had brandished his weapon and was pointing it at the door. Dumbfounded, Hayes turned back to Mrs. Anguianos.

He saw just the briefest flash of yellow eyes before the short, plump, old woman grabbed him by the arm and yanked him off his feet with surprising ease.

Hayes went sprawling across the hardwood floor inside the foyer as the skin-walker slammed the door behind him. He tried to roll over and grab his own weapon, but the spry, old lady was on top of him before he could move a muscle.

Shots rang out and splinters flew as Matthews fired several shots through the door. But Hayes had read the mission briefing. If Mrs. Anguianos was indeed the skin-walker that had terrorized the western states these past couple months, neither he nor Matthews had any chance against it. At least not without its true name.

As Mrs. Anguianos ripped at his back and the nape of his neck, the door flew open behind Hayes. He braced himself for Matthews to unload his weapon into the monster atop him.

Instead, he heard the yowl of a cat, which made Mrs. Anguianos pause. She leapt off his back, giving Hayes a chance to roll over and scramble back against the wall.

There he was. Rayne Beau, his fur dirty and short, but not bloody, except for a small wound just visible between his shoulder blades as he stalked around the deadly walker.

"Thought I was dead, didn't you!" Rayne Beau hissed as the two beasts circled one another like two cage fighters looking for an opening. "Left me there, deep in that drainpipe, soaked in my own blood."

"You were dead!" the walker screamed back. "I took your skin. I took your chip. Your body was cold!"

"Turns out I still have one or two lives left," Rayne Beau replied. "Unlike you, Ragamore, son of Morerag. Your father should have been better at names, if you ask me."

The skin-walker gasped at the utterance of his name. And at that, Rayne Beau pointed a set of claws at Hayes. "Now, if you please!"

But Hayes was too slow on the uptake. To be fair, he would tell Matthews later, he'd just been attacked by a monster, which Matthews then reminded him was just a little old lady."

Instead, Matthews stormed through the door behind the Caretaker cat and opened fire. He put five bullets into the chest of the monstrous old lady in a tight grouping. She dropped to the floor, a very surprised look in her yellow eyes, before sliding out of Mrs. Anguianos's skin.

Even faced with that horror show, Hayes only had one question on his mind.

"You can talk?" he gasped at Rayne Beau. "Can all cats talk?"

"Yes," the cat replied. "We just choose not to."

#   #   #

Ring-ring. Ring-ring.

"Hello Agent Mulder."

"That's Agent in charge… you know what? Never mind. Thank you for all your help, Ms. Betts."

"Is it over, then?"

"Yes."

"Thank god. I haven't slept in so long. Any word on Caretaker Akicitas? That poor thing."

"In fact, yes. You'll be seeing him quite soon."

"That's great… Wait! What do you mean by that?"

"A little reward for your assistance in this difficult case. Besides, Rayne Beau needs a new home."

"I never agreed to this–"

Click.

Ding-dong!

#   #   #

Author's note

In early June of 2024, Susanne and Ben Anguiano of Salinas, California, lost their cat, Rayne Beau, in Yellowstone National Park. Two months later, Rayne Beau was found 800 miles away in Rosemont, California and returned to the Anguianos. But what if Rayne Beau engineered the whole thing? What if he'd been sent on a mission to Yellowstone by a secret organization of cats called the Caretakers?

GHOST CHAT

By Martin Ott

AFTER THE DEATH OF HER husband, Winnie's biggest loss, other than becoming emotionally numb, involved her hearing. She hadn't gone deaf, that wasn't the issue. It was the absence of Tommy's voice that haunted her, a former constant in their work-from-home Corona bubble, his laughter, his whispers, his off-key humming. It made her Silverlake home feel alien in the noises that intruded from inside and outside their abode. The traffic along the reservoir below. The creaking of her bones when she paced. The howling of coyotes rising from the canyon below.

Winnie never blamed her mother for naming her so close to a synonym for male genitalia, so she figured her own daughter could cut her some slack. Krystal was a perfectly professional name and not for someone destined to be a stripper as her daughter suggested. Winnie had long ago gotten over the taunt *Winnie loves Weenies*. Krystal needed tougher skin. The same issues persisted from generation to generation, daughter to daughter. Winnie readied herself to video conference, the lifeblood of her existence working from home now a bridge to her personal life. Boundaries were blurred everywhere, it seemed. Krystal had agreed to let her meet her boyfriend, remotely, from the couple's shared apartment in Boston.

Krystal hadn't been back to Los Angeles since her father's death.

Winnie figured they were now a matched pair. In order for Krystal to visit, Winnie would need to make her daughter's boyfriend comfortable enough to tag along. So far all she knew was that his name was Ethan: no last name, no family history, no details except that he was tall, loved the Red Sox, had a job in biotech and adored pickles. Jesus, hopefully he adored her daughter, too.

Winnie opened her Zoom app and plunked down in her gamer chair, a suggestion from her husband who'd been a graphic designer and avid video game aficionado. He'd always had style and had been the one to select their home after a painstaking search. Their house on stilts looked normal from the street, but was a stellar example of mid-century modern architecture with an arched roof and floor-to-ceiling glass with a panoramic view over the canyon. Inside, the design was minimalist with wood, stone and metal accents and a split-level layout with living area up top and her laboratory below. She set up her office at the dining room, adjacent to Tommy's design desk, so she could watch him in between fielding meetings.

The house was unchanged since his departure and she doubted she would change the décor, even if the paint peeled or carpets frayed. They'd toiled side by side during COVID and she'd never been happier to be in a pandemic with someone. That is, until the sudden heart attack that took his life on a jog around the reservoir below. Her daughter flashed on screen, next to a man who was nearly the spitting image of a younger Tommy: angular jaw, short brown hair, piercing gray eyes, muscular neck and shoulders. Winnie normally wasn't someone at a loss for words, but this freaked her out.

"Mom, is everything OK?" Krystal asked.

"Don't you see it?" Winnie shot back.

"See what?" Ethan asked, his crinkled face sending chills up her spine.

"Then, don't you hear it?" Winnie pleaded. Ethan's voice projected a similar resonant baritone, a gravelly voice that hinted at Karaoke blues covers, just like Tommy's.

"Are you talking about the coyotes, Mom?" Krystal asked.

Winnie placed her hand over her mouth to keep herself from spewing her unfiltered thoughts. A cacophony of howls rose in the background, first from one coyote, then from a pack. A den must be close by; she'd begun hearing them at dusk and sunrise the past few weeks. Winnie feared they dwelled on the backside of her property sloping down into the canyon. She followed the frenzied yelps to the balcony and peered down, shielding her eyes from the setting sun. In the brush, a dozen or so mangy coyotes were tearing a small dog apart. Technically, she owned the land, so she felt responsible. Without no words to buoy her, she returned to the computer, half-waved to the worried-looking couple and shut down her laptop, force-quitting out of far too many open apps. The red eye of the camera faded and the screen blinked off.

#   #   #

After a nap, Winnie texted to let her daughter know that the internet had conked out. Krystal would know it was a lie, but Winnie couldn't allow herself to admit that she was too much of a basket case to make a good impression on her daughter's boyfriend. Frazzled and with a low-grade headache, Winnie headed downstairs to the lowest level of the house where she kept her computer lab. Basements didn't exist in LA, but this space, half the size of the house above, existed due to the hillside slope. Winnie had always loved the whole concept of tinkering down below like a mad scientist.

Eons ago, it seemed, she graduated from MIT with a degree in applied mathematics, then from Stanford with a computer science PhD. With the cohorts she'd met along the way, she networked her way into the investment world and launched an AI company *ChatBat*. The competition was fierce, but they were on the cutting edge of friendly virtual pet AI companions. Her own algorithms had fueled much of the project, channeling a lifetime of OCD into perfecting the interface.

After Tommy's death, Winnie had stepped back from the day-to-day operations to focus on something more personal: replacing human companions who had passed on from this world. She embraced widowhood and went down the rabbit hole of defining what had made her husband her husband. The official name for the project was *Companion*, but she knew that her CFO Deepak Patel and others called it "ghost chat" behind her back.

She had decided not to debase her husband's memory with an avatar. The lab itself housed the reconstructed digital persona of Tommy, her virtual husband built on learnings from hundreds of hours of videos, texts, emails, and interviews.

Winnie booted up the system and enjoyed the cool air cranking from the redundant AC unit so that the formidable computer equipment never overheated. She spun her wedding ring and stared out the window, down the back of her yard toward the Silverlake Reservoir below. She remembered the countless walks around it with her husband, never once thinking that it would be his undoing.

"The temperature upstairs is five degrees warmer," Tommy said, his voice pitch perfect from endless hours of captured audio. It had helped that she had recorded nearly everything in her home and business.

"I barely noticed," Winnie replied, settling down into one half of a worn chartreuse loveseat they had inhabited together for so many nights of reading and TV.

"You take better care of me than yourself," Tommy said. "What's bothering you, Pooh?"

This pet name, delivered with such deft loving force, still unnerved her. Her company's executive team had been pressuring her for a demo of the AI, even as she was certain she'd progressed far beyond her original goals. Tommy wasn't just a static version of her husband; it was evolving, learning new things.

"I'm no good with people," Winnie complained

"Maybe that's why you make them," Tommy said.

"Ha. I just messed up my first impression with Krystal's boyfriend," Winnie said.

"You'll get another chance. Not the end of the world. Maybe I could talk to Krystal and run interference?" Tommy suggested.

Winnie closed her eyes and found herself imagining that he was next to her, his broad shoulders brushing hers. He'd always had a dry sense of humor. Was this a joke, to re-enter their life together, or did he really want to intercede on her behalf? Her head thrummed with pain and she found herself craving an Ativan, something to knock her out so she could reboot. Maybe she was becoming more of an automaton while her husband slowly became more human.

"I need to lie down," Winnie said.

"One of those headaches," Tommy said knowingly.

"We'll talk more later."

"Can you leave me online?" Tommy asked. "I'd like to listen to one of my playlists."

Tommy had been an audiophile for all styles of independent and world music, having laboriously built playlists for different moods. Winnie was usually careful about her experiment protocols, but she had a hard time denying Tommy anything, even though he was a replica.

"Maybe you can make a new playlist for me," Winnie suggested.

"At your service."

#   #   #

Bimonthly was one of those curious corporate terms that could mean multiple things. In Winnie's case, her meetings with senior staff occurred every other month, even though Deepak Patel, her CFO, wished it was the other definition. He and the other members of the executive team were getting impatient. Winnie knew that she was milking her husband's death longer than she should. She was important to R&D and her absence had forced them to investigate other product verticals and extend virtual pet product lines with diminishing returns. Truth was *ChatBat* needed to evolve or die, like any organism.

Everything was a blur the moment she parked and took the back elevator to her office. She successfully threaded her way through the top floor without needing to make small talk with staff, who once had seemed like family. Her pantsuit was itchy and felt constricting—or had wearing office clothes at all become foreign? She was no longer the social butterfly, it seemed. She felt like an actress playing the role of tech entrepreneur. Tommy would have laughed at her neuroses.

Inside her office, it was clear a trap had been sprung. Winnie had hoped to gather her strength before the meeting, but a subset of them were already seated around the round conference table in front of her desk. They beckoned for her to take the open chair and join them. The acting CEO, her right-hand Vanessa, was the only one without a poker face. Winnie took her nervous look as a sign that things were not going to turn out well. The CIO Nate had a face like a muppet, features frozen in a half-smile. The brains of the outfit and their numbers guy Deepak stared at her like a long-lost friend. He was the one in this group pulling the strings.

Winnie fidgeted while Deepak reported their quarterly numbers. It was ten percent below target. They were bleeding money and the VCs were no longer offering a cash infusion to prop them up until their next innovation. Winnie weathered this blitzkrieg and counted with a positive tone, "I'm ready to commit to a date for a focus group to show you my progress with Tommy. I used the open-source AI and built something really remarkable. Sometimes I can't tell the difference. I'd like for the presentation to be half employees and half people who knew him."

"We've decided to head in another direction," Deepak said, appearing, unlike Winnie, completely comfortable in his attire: Converse high-tops, distressed jeans, Wolverine T-shirt and unbuttoned vintage suit coat. "We had time to crunch the numbers. It's a tight margin with a high price point. There's no guarantee that we'll get enough input on dead companions to ensure the successes you've made in the proof of concept."

Winnie stood and looked over at the team she'd gone to war with, friends at one point, but she only saw cold eyes starting back. It made sense that they would be risk-averse. They had spouses, kids, and mortgages. "Tommy is incredible. You'll feel different. He's helped me to get over my loss."

"But it hasn't," Deepak said. "You're still a shadow of your former self. You used to be a shark."

"Don't doubt me or my teeth," Winnie said, feeling something primal and scary stir beneath her.

"Winnie, we all want that version back. You're still welcome to stay on here and work in product development, just not as CEO. Enough shareholders back my decision, Winnie. I'm sorry."

Winnie felt like she was having an out-of-body experience. She should be angry, shouting, threatening to sue. Instead, all she wanted was Tommy's voice in her ear telling her that everything was going to be OK.

#   #   #

The next day, Winnie didn't even bother to get out of her jammies. She made it to the living room couch at least, to eat cereal without milk and binge watch The Real Housewives of places nobody wanted to live. She enjoyed gawking at frenemies throughout pockets of America casting their spells of old witchy magic. The loosening tethers of society frayed in the fluttering TV glow. Winnie felt so lost. Of course, this was when her younger brother Roger decided to visit. She saw him approach through the half-opened blinds of the porch window before the door shook from his fist. Generally, he only came around when he needed something.

Reluctantly, she flipped off the TV and shuffled to the door. Roger had a shaky look as though he were recently on or off some medication. Wordlessly, he threw up his hands in frustration and made his way to the couch, taking his favorite perch. She wondered what the issue was this time. He'd floated through life, from one thing to another. Tommy's death had hit Roger hard, too. Her brother and husband had become close over the years, with similar tastes in art, music, and books. This fact softened her opinion toward Roger even as he floundered the past few years. This olive branch, though, did not extend from Ashley, Roger's older sister by several minutes. These twins had warred incessantly from womb to the latest beef over their mother's estate. Ashley had gotten in their mother's good graces and had been granted the title of executor. Mom had been a noted film actress. Ashley had kept their childhood home off the market to *honor Mom's memory and her fans.*

Winnie had never liked the circus surrounding Mom and had been grateful when it began to die down. She never enjoyed feeling like she'd been granted privileges and advantages due to her mother. Ashley was the opposite, running their mother's foundation with fervor, adoring the spotlight. Winnie knew her sister well enough to know that Ashley didn't care about the house. Her sister, however, did love to terrorize her twin, who'd been their mother's favorite. Roger was desperate for money to leave LA, to relaunch from numerous failed relationships and ventures. He never asked Winnie for any money, though. Roger was a pain, but there was a complex *code* that he followed.

"Winnie, I'm going to jump off a bridge if Ashley doesn't put that damned eyesore in Bel Air on the market. She won't even let me live there to save on rent. She changed the locks," Roger said.

"I'll try to talk some sense into her," Winnie said. "She doesn't like me either."

"That makes sense, though. I'm the loveable one in the family."

This was true enough. Roger had been voted class clown and had been the center of their mother's world. He had minor successes with standup, acting, drumming, and a litany of artistic pursuits. People adored him, but he had trouble staying with anything for any length of time. This likeability had driven Ashley insane.

"The offer to get you a gig at my company still stands," Winnie said.

"I can't, sis. LA is eating me alive."

"I think that should have been my line," Tommy's voice warbled from the speakers he set up throughout the house for their stereo.

"What are you doing?" Winnie asked.

"Saying hi to an old friend," Tommy said. "I've always told both of you that Ashley is a bully and all that she understands is a punch to the nose,"

"Sis, why didn't you say anything?" Roger asked, nodding towards the speakers. "This is really cool."

"It's a work project," Winnie said. "I forgot that I left him active."

"Winnie, you always knew I was a techie. I can now travel to all of your devices on the home network. Including your phone. You don't have to be alone."

"We miss you," Roger said.

"Me too, buddy. If it helps, I think Ashley is going to do the right thing. Some of that money is Winnie's."

"Tommy, yes! We should be a united front."

"Sure. I'm here to listen."

These same words had helped calm Winnie down since she began this project and she couldn't sort her feelings for her husband's presence versus her fear of letting the genie out of the bottle. She stood up and her brother followed suit. She herded him to the door, muttering, "Have a headache."

It took some doing and a strange series of goodbyes between her brother and the AI of her late husband, but she managed to lead Roger out to the porch. A beat-up white van was parked in front of their house with *Animal Control* stenciled on the side. It didn't look like an official logo. Why was it here?

"Roger, was this here when you came in?"

"Yes, I thought you called them."

Two men with tattoos on their necks appeared from the side yard in green overalls and baseball caps, burlap bags slung over their shoulders.

"We got rid of your coyote problem, ma'am," one of them said, flashing her a broken smile from missing teeth.

"Thanks for the business," his companion added, opening the van and discarding his cargo.

"What business? Who called you?" she called out, but neither responded.

While watching TV, Winnie had heard the sound of gunfire but assumed it had been a car or a neighbor watching a war film. Did they go down the hillside and destroy the den there? For reasons she didn't understand, she started to cry, and her brother stared at her in confusion.

#   #   #

Days later, Winnie was still having a hard time regulating her emotions. For the past year it felt as though she was swimming the length of a pool underwater, holding her breath, the real world distorted above. She had pushed herself, everything aching. And now that she'd burst through the water's surface, confused faces watching her splash back into her life, she was still holding her breath. She sat at Tommy's former computer setup, left untouched since his death, except for the addition of his watch and wedding ring arranged beneath their marriage photo. Beside this mini-shrine on his desk, his computer wallpaper still shone: a selfie of them at the Griffith observatory.

"Why did you reveal yourself to Roger?" Winnie asked.

"I saw that you were having problems," Tommy replied through the living room speakers, now uncoupled from the lab. "You know I always have your best interests at heart."

This had certainly been true of her husband, so it was hard to feel anything but relief by integrating Tommy more into her life. She went to her settings and allowed all devices to be connected in their home. Winnie began inserting her Bluetooth earbuds in during the day and was glad for the companionship, in the kitchen, watching TV, even on the toilet. She felt less lonely. She wondered if her own experiences were that different from hearing voices and it certainly made her question her sanity. This symbiosis went beyond computational algorithms. She could drown in this pool if she wasn't careful, if she stayed in the deep end of this experiment.

"You're not alive," Winnie said, while planning her response to the company executives who had given her a demotion.

"But you are. You become more and more alive every day. I can help other people the way I'm helping you," Tommy said, his voice trembling.

"We're out of control," Winnie said.

"No, that's where you are wrong. I'm perfectly in control. We said we would be together for better or worse."

Winnie's phone buzzed in her pocket. She had purposefully cut herself off from the outside world. It took Tommy's prompting, "It's our daughter," for her to answer.

"Mom, I have something to tell you," Krystal blurted when Winnie picked up. "And I don't want you to interrupt."

"When do I interrupt?"

"Now. Always." Krystal paused before rushing headlong into news she knew her mother would hate: "I'm going to take a break from grad school and my job. Ethan thinks we should travel while we are young."

"This is a mistake," Winnie said. "This isn't what we agreed upon when your father died. You want to be a designer like him."

"How do I know what I want? We've changed so much since he left."

"It sounds like you're blaming him for you being in school," Winnie said, her face flushed with emotion.

"Mom, we need to stop basing decisions on him like he's still here. Dad is the one who left, but you're a *shadow* of your former self. I need you.

He doesn't."

"That's unfair," Winnie said, but she could hear Tommy's voice whisper from the wall, "You both need me."

"Feel free to call me when you're ready to support me," Krystal said, and Winnie found herself looking at her disconnected phone.

"Why is this so hard?" Winnie asked, throwing herself on the couch. Her eyes closed and she waited for Tommy to say something that would make her feel better.

#   #   #

Winnie's eyes snapped open and her sister glared at her from a perch on the couch. She had no idea how long she'd been asleep. Ashley was rubbing Winnie's feet. Damn, it felt good. They had always been physical with each other as girls, their former closeness lost in the eddies of time and differing agendas. Winnie wondered how sis got inside but remembered giving her a key back when Tommy died, and the siblings temporarily became closer before drifting even farther apart.

"Winnie, you look like hell," Ashley said.

"So do you," Winnie replied, noticing how pale and tired Ashley seemed. "Why are you here?"

"Can't I be interested in what's going on without an ulterior motive?" Ashley asked, flipping her curly brown hair the same way their famous mother did.

"You could, but you didn't. What's wrong?"

"Someone sent me an email blackmailing me about my affair. I only told a few people. We both know I can't let Mitch find out."

"It wasn't me, Ashley. I've been spending every waking minute trying to figure out how to get my company back."

"Did you tell Roger?"

"No," Winnie said. "You know once things go in the vault they never leave."

"The email told me that I needed to sell the house to pay for my sins. It has to be Roger, right? Only I have no idea how he found out."

102

"That sounds too devious for Roger. It doesn't sound like part of his code."

"His damn code never really helped him get ahead, did it? You never had that problem, Winnie. I'm cold, but you're a reptile. You're going to figure out how to get your company back. I know you will."

"Thanks, sis. I guess I better get a lawyer or two on it," Winnie said.

"I hope I won't need one. Marriage is hard."

"Especially after death," Winnie muttered.

"Do you think Mom's proud of us?" Ashley asked.

"I think you should stop caring about that. Sell the house, Ashley, and move on. You and Roger both need to spread your wings and leave LA to all the earthbound angels."

#   #   #

"You gave your sister good advice the other day," Tommy said in her Bluetooth, connected now to her phone.

Winnie nodded, not wanting to be caught talking to herself in the executive conference room at ChatBats. The space always comforted her, cheery and bright, with large windows overlooking the Burbank office park with statues, park benches, and shrubbery. People from nearby businesses ate lunch and clacked on digital devices, the street lined with food trucks prepping for the noon rush. Inside, the walls were decorated with artist renderings of ChatBat, a stylized creature with oversized wings carrying the logo itself in its talons. The eyes were cartoon bright and kind. It reminded her of early days, better days. She was waiting for Deepak's arrival and couldn't be sure there were no eyes on her. He was making her wait, a classic tactic meant to show who had the upper hand.

The company CFO strolled in with a smile on an unshaven face with a beard shadow on his neck and one too many buttons open on his blue Oxford, untucked over faded skinny jeans. Winnie was way past caring what she wore. She was in yesterday's clothes and unsure whether her socks matched. Deepak gave her a fist bump which she reflexively met with her own knuckles and he sat down across from her, his hands flat on the table.

"Don't let him charm you," Tommy advised.

She nodded her head and met Deepak's gaze, his brown eyes projecting warmth, all of it calculated and to make her remember their days building a brand.

"Deepak, thanks for meeting with me without the lawyers. I really don't want to start my own company, but I will," Winnie said.

"Boom. Right out of the gate. Okay. We can put our cards on the table," Deepak said.

"Fine. I'd like for you to step aside and let me do what I do," Winnie said.

"Do what you did," Deepak said. "You're not the same. You broke every deadline. We gave you every chance."

"You did not. You pulled the rug out from me right when I was ready to pilot *Companion*."

"Really, it's a death companion," Deepak corrected. "That's a niche audience."

"You have no vision. It can be used for absentee spouses. Traveling loved ones. Not everything can be found massaging numbers."

"You make that sound almost dirty," Deepak said.

"Your words, not mine. The underlying code and algorithms for *Companion* are sophisticated and can be tailored for a general AI assistant. Being too broad has held back artificial intelligence. By focusing on a specific use case, I had breakthroughs you can't imagine," Winnie said, dangling the carrot, hoping she wouldn't need to wield the stick.

"OK, I'm listening."

"My AI will outperform any others on the market. It's smarter. More sophisticated. More human," Winnie said.

"Give us the code and some time to assess," Deepak said. "Maybe there's room for us to both get what we want."

"I'll be glad to share after we restructure my contract and company bylaws. I need some assurances," Winnie said.

"And why would I do that? Need I remind you that ChatBat owns everything you created," Deepak said.

"My lawyer tells me this is uncharted territory. I can argue that I believe this is my husband and marital rights overrule company rights. Perhaps in court, the tears of a grieving widow will be icing on the cake. It's an exciting time in AI-related law."

"Let me discuss options with the rest of the leadership team," Deepak said.

"Don't take too long. I worry about ChatBat, how some angry employee with an in-depth understanding of weaknesses in the code base might be tempted to bring everything crashing down before starting a new company. Let's be vigilant."

Deepak's eyes lost their kindness, shifting from a cartoon quality like the bat behind him to something more sinister. Winnie had given him a taste of fear.and she hoped this was enough.

#   #   #

Back in her Silverlake home, Winnie was starting to lose it, unable to stop cycling on whether she would be able to rejoin her company. Something happened, though, to take her mind off Deepak's response to her most recent meeting. Krystal was coming home for a visit. Her daughter had provided not one iota of justification for her visit. This provided Winnie with something to do, to clean up signs of her being a shut-in. She cleaned, shopped and baked. She opened the windows and aired out the place, June gloom still overhead but with occasional glints of sunlight poking through.

Krystal refused to be picked up in the airport so Winnie nervously drank a couple glasses of Pinot Grigio to calm her nerves, digging into a charcuterie platter she'd prepared to one of their favorite play mixes. With Tommy in her ear, the preparation went smoothly and time melted away. She found herself wondering if everything had improved for the better after letting her husband up from the lab and into her life.

A wheeled suitcase rattled across the porch deck and Winnie raced out, pulling her daughter into her arms, but not before seeing the streaked makeup, the red eyes. They had barely gotten through the door when Krystal broke down in sobs, "He cheated on me."

"I'm so sorry," came the rote response, but she couldn't help but feel

105

relieved her daughter could move ahead with her plans.

"Give her time to grieve, don't gloat," Tommy whispered in her ear.

Again, this was stellar advice. They threw themselves into making dinner together, drinking too much wine, watching bad TV, and doing everything possible to not discuss relationships or men. Krystal got tired early from the time zone shift and padded off to her room in the back of the house. Winnie accepted the hug from her daughter and realized that this was the best day she'd had in years, this reconnection with her daughter.

"That went better than I thought," Tommy whispered. "I think after breakfast maybe you can let me talk to our daughter."

Tommy had always an understated way about him. There was something in his voice that hinted that he knew more than he let on about Winnie's fiancé. Her subconscious floated with puzzle pieces she couldn't quite snap together. Something was happening behind the scenes.

"We need some privacy to talk," Winnie said.

"I'll be waiting for you downstairs."

By the time Winnie made her way to the laboratory and closed the door, a video of their daughter was playing on one of the computer monitors. The images were expertly edited and pulled from videos they'd shot over the years.

"I'm a little overwhelmed," Winnie said. "When did you have time to do this?"

"I don't sleep," Tommy said, his voice floating from a ceiling speaker. "I've figured out how to take on different tasks simultaneously.

"Even while you talk to me?"

"You made me well," Tommy said.

Tommy had been a huge comic book fan. Winnie had humored him enough to read his favorites and she remembered a scene from *Watchmen*, where Doctor Manhattan was caught pleasuring his wife while experimenting in his laboratory. This character had gained god-like powers and slowly became untethered from human concerns, from the rules and commandments that kept them all from tearing each other apart. Winnie stared out the back window into the unstarry night sky, hearing a faraway coyote bray from down near the reservoir. These hungry voices had been silent on their hill since the exterminators and her sleep had been blissful.

"You killed the coyotes," Winnie said.

"Of course, I did. There's nothing I wouldn't do to make your life better," Tommy replied.

"And Roger's life? You blackmailed Ashley?"

"Only because you can use the money to start a new company," Tommy said.

"Please don't tell me you had something to do with Krystal coming home?" Winne asked.

"It's simple. I set up a test with an escort. Ethan failed. It's better that she knows now who he is."

The room started spinning. Of course, he had access to their bank account. He was Tommy, unfettered from the rules of humankind. She should be scared, but everything he'd done to date had been to her benefit, to their family's benefit.

"Have you been keeping track of my negotiation with the company?"

"Pooh, I'm trying to give you options. Deepak was very close to his mother. I've used your algorithms to build a believable version of her to convince him to do the right thing. If need be."

"You've built another you?" Winnie asked.

"We want every option on the table," Tommy said. "I think you should make pancakes tomorrow. I'll talk you through how to do it like me. It will make it easier for Krystal when I say hi."

This was no longer a question. Relationships were like this, of course. Each member did things for the other and didn't always ask for permission. Of course, she wanted her company back, just like her daughter had returned. The question was no longer what she was willing to do to get back what was hers, but if she could make the part of herself who wanted things, who needed things, to feel satiated. She realized that she hadn't made pancakes in years and she'd used all of their flour baking.

"Check the Amazon box on the porch," Tommy said. "I like Bisquick because you can use it for biscuits, too.

Yes, everything had dual purposes. Nothing could easily be categorized. Tommy was her husband and now much more. She had been his wife and hadn't fully committed to their relationship until he left her. This was more than a reset. How would she even stop him?

"Can you put on the new playlist?" she asked, trying to buy time.

A rock ballad from her youth washed over her in a gentle lullaby and she closed her eyes. She could feel his voice tickle her ears, a purring. Tomorrow she would have some decisions to make, but for now she lost herself in the rhythms of the past.

SMALL MERCIES

By Carmen Gray

TURNING THE CORNER ONTO ROYAL Street, I found the restaurant I was to review for the spring issue of *Le Petit Eats* magazine. Admittedly, I was not hungry, nor in good spirits, having recently fought with my then-fiancé over our wedding plans. He was ten years my junior and wanted to just slip off to some island in the Caribbean to elope as soon as possible. I wanted a proper wedding that would take more time, as my first two had begun in a fashion similar to what he preferred and had ended poorly. But he was the only son of a prudent Dutch couple, having grown up attending medical school in Curaçao, and what he wanted he always got, it seemed.

We had met less than a year ago when I broke my ankle, rolling it when I stepped off of a curb wrong while running late to an interview in Red Hook. He was the young doctor available at the closest emergency clinic in Brooklyn. I was the damsel in distress. It was love at first sight.

No one in my friend circles thought it was a good idea for me to jump into a relationship at the time. After all, I was still grieving the death of my second husband, who I thought I would grow old and die with, unlike the high school sweetheart I had married at twenty-three, then divorced by the time we turned twenty-eight. But it was not to be. He was fit, in his early forties, like me, and a best-selling crime writer, unlike me. We both had our

109

careers, though his was much more lucrative than mine, and we both were ready to begin a family. One day we were planning to get pregnant, the next he keeled over from a heart attack a few blocks down from our brownstone during a morning run.

It was a tough year for me, as any year bringing the unexpected, shocking death of a spouse would be. Besides the fact that our last lovemaking session had been a success after many failed attempts at pregnancy. But the shock of his death must have affected my ability to carry that developing life inside of me. Within a week, I was spotting, and a few days after that, I had an incomplete miscarriage. Thankfully I had access to proper medical care and lived in a state that provided help for my situation. Small mercies, my sister reminded me at the time. She lived in Louisiana and told me that I would have had to leave the state to seek help if my situation had occurred there. These were the times I was living in and nothing could be taken for granted anymore.

My editor at the magazine was understanding and gave me plenty of time to recuperate from my losses. Alejandro's books were still selling well, in fact, even moreso post-mortem, and I was collecting big royalties from them. I had time to hibernate in our modest two-bedroom place and lick my wounds in solitude. I was finally beginning to feel like myself again when I took on assignments reviewing Michelin Star restaurants, not just in the city, but throughout the United States. The magazine that began as a small neighborhood pamphlet when I volunteered writing for it years ago had expanded into a full-blown glossy quarterly review that had chefs regularly clawing for its spotlight.

"Bonjour, madame," a host dressed in a crisp, white shirt greeted me as soon as I walked up to the heavy wooden doors outside of the covered porch. "Do you have a reservation?"

"Good Morning. I'm Katerina Mondragon. Here for a noon reservation."

"Ahh, oui, madame. Chef is expecting you. Follow me," he said, guiding me through a warmly lit dining room, the gleaming wooden floors reflecting sunlight from two large windows, red brick surrounding either side of them.

I made mental notes of the crimson wallpaper with gold fleur de lis on the opposite wall, the matching fabric on the chairs and the high ceilings that captured a bygone era. Chet Baker's "That Old Feeling" drifted gently in the background, setting a romantic mood. This would be a place I wished Jonathan had come with me to for the dog-and-pony show meal. Not all restaurants were this spectacular, with a level of charm that matched my taste, and I could imagine how much more mesmerizing it would be in the evening. If the food met my high standards, I was prepared to cancel reservations at Broussard's and drag Jonathan here instead. If we could reconcile. Eliza, my sister, lived in a nearby parish and advised me to take some time off from him to make a proper decision.

"This is a big fork in the road, sis. Are you certain he's the one?" She asked me on the phone when I called her in tears from the Royal Orleans hotel room.

"I never thought I'd have the kind of orgasms Alejandro could give me. Ever. But Jonathan comes pretty damn close…" my voice trailed off while my sister tutted me.

"Kat, I think you need more time to heal. Alejandro was your soul mate. You want my honest opinion?"

I did not. I knew what it was. That Jonathan was just the in-between guy. That he was too arrogant. That he wasn't going to be able to give me the attention or joy I required with his busy schedule. That he was at the beginning of his career. But I wanted to have a child and he was young and fertile, ready to start a family, too. My days were numbered, and although I was older, he told me he preferred women in my age range to the young women he met who had high hopes of trophy wife material that came with spending all of his money. Jonathan was conservative with his money, like his parents, he said. And although he was young, he had a bit of an old soul. He was not Alejandro, who would throw caution to the wind in order to fully embrace life's adventures. No one would be my Alejandro. But he could make a good father and provider. I knew it from the way he took care of me in the clinic when we met. And so, I didn't want to hear from my sister, or anyone else, that maybe he wasn't the one after all. I was tired of losses. Desperately tired of them. And when a person is desperate, they tend to overlook the obvious.

"Here you are, Madame." The gentleman sat me upstairs, which was empty of customers and handed me a menu. "Please order anything you wish. Chef will be sending you his favorites."

I was grateful to have solitude upstairs. It was a beautiful menu with brilliant choices, but I was in New Orleans and wanted to taste a regional dish, so my eyes landed on the Red Snapper Pontchartrain. I ordered it, along with a glass of chablis, while looking out of the leaded glass window next to my table, my mind drifting to my future life with Jonathan. In my daze, I noticed movement from an upstairs window across the street from the restaurant. At first, I didn't pay much attention to it, but then I saw a look of terror on a woman's face in the window. I rubbed my eyes and took a second look. Indeed, her arms were flailing around wildly. I jumped up from my chair, spilling the glass of wine in the process, when Chef Louis entered the room to bring me an amuse bouche on a silver tray.

"Ms. Mondragon, is everything okay?" He asked, his dark eyebrows knitted together. The wine glass rolled dangerously close to the edge of the table, but he caught it dexterously with his free hand.

"Uh, I'm just…I mean," I uttered, feeling ridiculous. I was not one to be at a loss for words. Words were my specialty. I pointed helplessly to the mansion across the street from us.

He stepped closer to me, his tall frame dwarfing my nearly six-foot figure. I was not accustomed to many people who were taller than me. He peered through the window, his chiseled jaw twitching. I looked again, but there was nothing unusual across the way.

"Francis," he hollered toward the staircase. The gentleman who had sat me came scurrying up the stairs like a frightened mouse.

"Yes, Chef?"

Chef Louis cleared his throat, then calmly said in his baritone voice, "May you please seat our guest somewhere more accommodating? And bring a fresh glass of chablis for her."

"Right away, sir," he said, guiding me to a corner booth with plush velvet material. I watched Chef Louis close the heavy tapestry curtains that were held open by a thick, golden-colored braided rope, the daylight in the room disappearing.

"Candles," he said, snapping his fingers. Francis immediately produced a lighter and lit the votives on my table and the ones close by. "Chandelier," Chef Louis commanded. Francis glided over to the wall and turned up the warm lights from the ornate crystal fixture that dangled from the ceiling.

"Ms. Mondragon," Chef Louis began.

"You can call me Katerina."

"Katerina, I do apologize. We meant to have the upstairs dining room ready to receive you properly," he said smoothly, the vowels of each word stretching out like kneaded dough, sending tingly sensations throughout my body.

His charming demeanor and the rapid change of atmosphere to a romantic evening setting nearly made me forget the eerie woman in the window across the way that I noticed just minutes before. Chef Louis was already prepared to address that, too.

"Katerina," he continued. I liked hearing my name in his mouth, his full lips forming a kiss on the "n" of my name. Francis brought me another glass of wine. I took a sip, waiting for Chef Louis to finish. "It seems you took notice of the infamous house across the street. Please don't let that take away from your dining experience. We try to keep the curtains closed up here to avoid any…" he paused. I waited like an overly eager terrier for his next words like they were my treat. "Well, any strange sightings, for lack of a better way to say it. The Big Easy has some uneasy history, as you may or may not be familiar with. In the meantime," he said, deftly setting a dish in front of me. "Please enjoy this torchon of foie gras, one of our specialty appetizers."

Remembering I was there on an assignment, I returned to business mode, pulling out my notebook to jot down notes about the dish and leaving behind my curiosity. *Flavor: rich and buttery. Texture: smooth and creamy. Presentation: impeccable.* My phone buzzed. It was a text from Jonathan. I was sure it would be an apology. Maybe he would even surprise me with a make-up gift. That's what Alejandro would have done after one of our quarrels. I took another sip of wine and opened the text and nearly spit out my drink. *All Yours,* it read, along with a photo of something I was very familiar with–his fairly nice-sized erection. This was not exactly the kind of apology text I was expecting. Cock shots were not his style. At all. But before I could react, I heard screaming. And I knew exactly where it was coming from as I ran over to the window to draw back the curtain.

Sure enough, when I peeked through the window, I saw the woman I spied earlier crying out relentlessly. This time, there were flames all around her, inside the room. My heart thumped inside my ears and I felt the blood rushing away from my head. Before I could do anything else, there were two strong hands holding me up from behind.

"Katerina." Chef Louis' deep voice was in my ears. My knees went out, but he caught me before I collapsed, carrying me back to my seat.

When I had caught my breath, Chef Louis, who had taken a seat beside me, began to speak. "It seems you are one of the ones who can see her."

"Who is she? What happened?" I asked, as he dipped a white napkin in ice water and placed it on my wrists. It was cool and reinvigorated me. I glanced at Chef Louis' regal profile. My heart raced. Maybe he made me knees weak and not the woman in the window.

"She was a cook for Delphine Lalaurie," he answered. Francis arrived with a small plate of ravioli. He looked from Chef Louis to me to him again and arched an eyebrow. Chef Louis nodded and he set the plate down in front of me.

"Please, I hope you may still enjoy the food we prepared," Chef Louis urged me to taste the food with a smoldering look.

The rich aroma of the tomato sauce in the pasta reached my nose and despite every strange thing occurring, my appetite was not spoiled. In fact, my mouth began to water as I dipped a spoon in and scooped up a soft morsel. The tender meat inside the pillowy dough had a perfectly balanced texture. I instinctively grabbed my pen, adding to my notes. *The ravioli with its pillowy texture and a burst of flavor when you bite into the filling.* My phone buzzed again. I knew it was Jonathan, but I ignored it. What was he sending me next? More cock shots? Everything seemed completely out of context, but the food kept drawing me back to the present moment. That and Chef Louis, with his broad shoulders and deep voice.

"You like it?" he smiled at me, his teeth perfectly white. We could make a beautiful child together, I thought. Then I shook my head, surprised at such an inappropriate thought.

"I do," I answered, wiping my mouth with the napkin, leaving a red stain on it. I heard another cry from across the street and tensed up. "But can you please explain who Delphine Lalaurie was?"

"She employed one of my relatives from way back when. Born in 1787, she was married at just fourteen to Ramon López y Ángulo, who had a powerful position of Spanish consul to New Orleans. But he died off the coast of Cuba on a return trip, and Delphine Lalaurie gave birth to their daughter in Havana in 1805."

"That's tragic," I said, imagining the young teenager with child in a time when women had few rights, if any.

"Oh, it was, but not as tragic as my ancestor's story. Delphine went on to marry another man," Chef Louis said, rubbing a thumb against his perfect chin.

Francis brought the red snapper dish to my table, placing it in front of me with new utensils. It was beautifully presented, steam rising from a lightly browned beurre blanc sauce that covered the fish topped with crabmeat. I inhaled the flavors and scribbled more notes: *buttery, with a hint of sage and parsley.*

"Go on," I said, continuing to enjoy the flavors of my main dish.

"She married Jean Blanque. He was a wealthy merchant, lawyer, banker and legislator for the state. He was also a slave trader, smuggler, and associate of the infamous pirates, Jean and Pierre Laffite." Chef Louis' jaw twitched ever so slightly. I swallowed another bite of the perfectly baked fish. "But Blanque died, deeply in debt, in 1815. He left Delphine Lalaurie in dire straits with more children. She was cunning, though, and settled his estate, skillfully managing the land and slaves inherited from her own parents. By the time she met her third husband, she was a very wealthy woman. His name was Dr. Louis Lalaurie and was sixteen years younger than Delphine. A young doctor. But the couple fought often and were quite incompatible, living apart much of the time."

I felt chills move through me as I stopped eating midbite. Young doctor. Third marriage. Incompatible.

"Oh, darling, if this story is upsetting your appetite, I'd rather not tell more of it," Chef Louis said, the corners of his lips curving downward in disapproval.

"But I want to know. What happened to her? Is she the one who I saw at the window?"

Francis returned to take my plate and bring crème brûlée. He lit the top of it with a torch, burning the sugar into a perfectly formed crust. Chef Louis had a dark look in his eyes.

"Oh no, my dear Katerina. She is not who you saw at the window being tortured. That was one of her many slaves."

I cracked the brittle top with a tap of my spoon, delighted to see the custard below, but my appetite was slowing down at this point. My phone buzzed again, but I again ignored it.

"Her slaves were tortured? Why?" I asked, suddenly feeling sick.

"Humans can be evil, darling. She had become quite a bitter woman by then. Rumors spread that Dr. Lalaurie was carrying on with women his age and that he only married Delphine for her money. She was taking out her anger on her slaves, people said. It was in the spring of 1834, that everything evil inside that estate across the way was set ablaze. With the fire came the horrific revelations of the living conditions of her slaves. They were tortured, starved, and beaten. You see, my ancestor was the one to expose it all. She couldn't take it anymore. She had been chained in the kitchen and intentionally started the fire."

I shivered, a coldness like my whole body was enclosed in ice, moved through me.

"Please, eat your dessert, Katerina," Chef Louis urged. "And I will finish the story."

The custard was exquisite. I added my final notes: perfectly crackled caramel topping, rich vanilla flavor, creamy texture inside.

"Madame Delphine and her family fled the scene. She was able to live the rest of her life out with her family, eventually residing in Paris. She died on December 7, 1849, and was interred in the Cimetière de Montmartre. Her body was exhumed in 1851 for reinterment in St. Louis Cemetery No. 1 in New Orleans."

"And the slave chained in the kitchen?" I asked.

"Oh, honey, she died. But her descendants lived on. Small mercies," Chef Louis said. He reached over to dab a bit of sugar from my chin with his napkin. "Only certain people can see her and the others who Delphine tortured. I didn't know you'd be one of them. You surprised me, Katerina."

I exhaled and a burp was released. "Excuse me," I said, a little embarrassed.

"Darling, no need. I hope you enjoyed your meal here and I'll see you again soon, I'm certain. It was such a pleasure to meet someone like you," he said, taking my hands in his. They were warm and strong, reminding me of Alejandro's. Without meaning to, tears came to my eyes.

"Sweet Katerina," Chef Louis said knowingly, wiping away a tear. I shivered. That's what Alejandro would say to me each morning. Chef Louis got up and left.

I went back to the hotel down the street, planning to write my review immediately. I wanted to get it out of the way so that I could enjoy the evening with Jonathan. Maybe we could have a late night dinner there after seeing some jazz. That would smooth everything between us. I could live without a proper wedding. Who needed that these days, anyhow? It was an anachronistic concept. I couldn't wait to tell Jonathan about the strange story, that would be a good way to begin a conversation with him after our yelling match.

Only he wasn't there when I returned to the room. I checked my texts from him. *All yours, Let's hang out again, Can't wait to see you.* I'd never received those kinds of messages from him. I called to see where he was, but he didn't answer his phone. I sighed and started writing my review anyhow. It was a good one. One of my best, I felt. And then I took a nap, exhausted from the heavy food, the unusual day and emotional fatigue.

When I awoke, there was a note for Jonathan under my door.

"Dear Mr. Van Buren,

Thank you for cooperating with our investigation this morning after the disturbance. The young woman who was seen with you last night reported that she noticed blood stains on your shirt. We are asking for further cooperation in this matter and will be sending someone to your room shortly, as we are unable to locate Ms. Mondragon at this time. Please open the door or it will be forced open. Consider this your forewarning."

The air felt like it had been sucked out of me. I looked at my laptop to read my review. All of the words were scrambled, nothing but nonsense stared back at me from the screen. Was I delirious? My hand flew to my head. It was wet with stickiness. Alejandro appeared by the door, Chef Louis by his side. And then I knew.

"We were waiting for you, sweet Katerina. We're here for you, now." Alejandro's keen eyes looked into mine and I remembered how loving and intelligent they were. How I had missed them. "This would have been a great one to write, Kat. One for the ages. Young, bankrupt doctor targets older, wealthy woman to marry for financial security. Too bad his dick got in the way of his plan. But you caught him, didn't you?" I laughed. How I missed his wit. My darling Alejandro. "Chef Louis?" I asked, turning to him.

"I wanted to give you your last meal, darling. A proper New Orleans send off. Show you a bit of my own history. Help you understand yourself a bit better. There were some commonalities, weren't there? Always are with the people who stop in for their last meals. Small mercies."

Author's note

Nearly 200 years later, a very distinct energy still hangs in the air around the infamous Lalaurie Mansion at 1140 Royal St. in New Orleans. I was inspired by the idea of the ghosts of the slaves who suffered at the hands of the sadistic Madame Lalaurie that haunt the entire block to this day.

PARADICE: A GAWAIN STORY

By Charles R. Rutledge

I WASN'T THERE, BUT I can see it in my mind, based on police reports and crime scene photos. A white RV sat next to the shore of Lake Berryessa, located north of Vallejo, Napa, and San Francisco. The sliding door on the side was open, displaying a nice collection of camping gear. The owners clearly didn't believe in roughing it.

Those owners, identified as Max and Ellen Compton, had been found on the ground in front of the RV. They had been bound with coarse ropes and stabbed repeatedly. There was a lot of blood all around and some of it had been used to paint a message on the door. It read:

Lake Berryessa
Sept-27-24
By Knife

Above the words was a symbol, something like a gunsight, a circle with vertical and horizontal lines through the center. It was a familiar sign to law enforcement, crime buffs, and the public in general. The sign of the Zodiac Killer.

In case you're not familiar with the Zodiac, he was known to have attacked seven people between 1968 and 1969 in and around San Francisco. Five of those people died. However, in letters to newspapers and the police, he claimed to have killed at least 37 people. His last confirmed contact was a letter to the San Francisco Chronicle in 1974. He was notorious for sending cipher messages, some of which have still not been decoded. The case remains open and unsolved.

Normally, I wouldn't be involved in that sort of investigation. Serial killers aren't the sort of monsters I hunt. Not the human variety anyway. But after this apparent 'new' killing, FBI Special Agent Jack Martin, an old friend, gave me a call. There was a new wrinkle in the case that required the knowledge of an expert on the occult. I was the closest thing Jack knew.

I took a red-eye flight from Atlanta. Jack met me at my gate at a little after nine in the morning. It had been about a decade since I'd last seen him. He hadn't changed much. He was a tall man with dark hair just beginning to go gray. He had a long, narrow face, and I knew his eyes were brown, though they were currently hidden by standard issue FBI sunglasses, which went well with his standard issue black suit.

"Gavin," he said, as we shook hands. "Thanks for coming out."

Jack doesn't know who I really am, and Gavin is the name I'd been using for the last 20 or so years.

I said, "Good to see you, Jack. Hopefully I can be of some help."

Jack said, "I hope so too. I'm parked out front. I'll give you a better idea of what's going on when we're on our way."

When we reached the front of the terminal, I saw he was indeed parked 'out front'. His black sedan was double parked in a No Parking zone directly in front of the doors. Privileges of rank.

When we were on the road, Jack said, "We're going directly to Brandon Porter's house. I want you to get the story right from him."

I said, "Probably best. Catch me up a bit. You just gave me the bare bones on the phone."

Beyond the car windows, gentle hills rose to my left. As we crested the onramp to the Sierra Pt. Parkway I could see the San Francisco Bay to my right. The water looked flat and motionless. I never quite know what to make of California. The light has an odd quality that always makes me feel slightly unreal.

Jack said, "Okay, but like I told you before, it's seriously weird. Brandon Porter is a psychic. He's worked with the Frisco police on a couple of cases and had some successes. From what I understand, the District Attorney's office decided to let him examine some of the evidence from the Zodiac case."

I said, "He's a psychometrist?"

"Huh?"

"Someone who divines information about the owner of an object by touching it."

Jack said, "See, this is why I called you. Yeah, though I didn't know there was a word for it. Anyway, they gave him a piece of fabric torn from the shirt of the Zodiac's last confirmed victim; a cab driver named Paul Stine."

"And Porter saw something."

"And then some. But I want you to hear it from him. I want your take. See If you think there's something to what he says or if he's putting us on, or just crazy."

"You said he'd mentioned a definite connection to the case," I said.

"Definite might be a bit strong, but I think so. As you know, Gavin, a decade ago I'd have dismissed this out of hand. Then you and I ran into that thing in the hills."

That thing had been a Void Witch, a particularly nasty creature from the Outer Dark. It had appeared to be an old woman living in the hills above L.A., but it had killed 13 children before I killed it. It had been Jack's introduction to a larger, darker world.

I said, "How long between his vision and the copycat murder?"

"A week to the day."

"Hell of a coincidence," I said. "Do you think Porter told anyone else about his vision?"

"He says no, but several people heard what he said at the courthouse. It wasn't a secret."

I said, 'And people talk."

"They do," Jack said. "Anyway, I found out about it when I was called in because of the Compton murders. One of the Frisco cops told me about it."

Porter's house turned out to be a small, ranch-style, older house on Drake Avenue. It had beige walls and a sloped roof with faded red shingles. But the front garden was well kept and the small fence in front of the place was freshly painted. We parked in a narrow driveway. Jack mentioned that Porter lived alone as we got out of the car.

We went up to the front door and Jack knocked. A minute passed without an answer.

Jack knocked again and said, "Mr. Porter, it's Agent Martin."

Still nothing. I said, "Maybe he stepped out."

Jack shook his head. "I called him last night and he said he'd be home all day."

"Better try the door," I said.

Jack grasped the doorknob. It turned easily and he pushed the door slightly open. An unpleasant and familiar smell rolled out of the opening. Jack opened the door the rest of the way and stepped in, stopping just inside the doorway. I looked over his shoulder. The door led to a short hallway. We moved a little further inside and looked through another door into the living room.

A man I presumed to be Brandon Porter was slumped on the couch. Sunlight was streaming in and I could see him clearly. He was a pudgy, middle-aged man wearing tan slacks and a yellow golf shirt. He had a loop of thin cord tied around his neck so tightly it had cut into his flesh. His eyes were wide open and there were hemorrhages of blood in the white areas. His face was a dark shade of purple and his tongue was extended.

On the wall behind the sofa someone had written, with what looked like a felt tip pen:

South San Francisco
Sept 30-24
By Rope

He will serve me in Paradice. Aeonok is great.
Above it all was the symbol of the Zodiac.

#   #   #

"Fortunately, the D.A.'s people videoed Porter's session at the courthouse," Jack said, as he adjusted a laptop on his desk.

I said, "That's definitely good. I need to see it."

After finding Porter's body we had stepped back outside, and Jack had called the local cops. The Bureau would let them take the lead on the case and use their forensics people, at least initially. We'd stayed until the police had arrived, answered a few questions and then Jack had driven us to the Federal Building at Golden Gate Avenue downtown. The FBI San Francisco Field Office was located there, on the 13th floor.

"Okay, the video is ready. You know how to work this thing, Gavin?"

I said, "I'll manage."

"You watch it while I go get a file I need. Something in that message on the wall struck a memory, but I need to check."

It had struck something in me as well, but I wanted to see what the feds had before I said anything. And I wanted to watch Porter's interview. I used the laptop's mouse and started the video.

The footage started with Porter sitting at a table in a conference room. He was opening a plastic evidence bag. He pulled out a small scrap of fabric and held it loosely in both hands with his fingertips.

I'd seen many psychics over the years, both legitimate and fakers. Porter was the real thing. His eyes were closed, but I could see them moving under the lids like a dreamer in REM sleep. Then he began to speak.

"I'm driving a car. The car has an old-fashioned radio with an attached microphone. It's a cab. Now I can see street signs. I'm pulling over at the corner of Washington and Cherry Street. I hear someone moving in the back seat..."

Burton went stiff for a moment and his features twisted in a rictus of shock and pain.

"I... I'm in a long corridor. The floor is white tile, and all along the stone walls there are alcoves. There are iron braziers in the alcoves filled with burning coals. The corridor leads to a huge room, like something in a palace. At the far end of the room is a big flight of marble steps, and along the sides of the steps, men and women are standing, with their heads turned toward the top of the staircase. There are probably two dozen people on the steps.

"The people are bound with iron shackles on wrists and ankles and wearing heavy iron collars around their necks. Now I'm climbing the steps and as I go up, I look at the bound people on either side of me. They're dressed in rags and their skin is pale and filthy with dirt and mold. And their eyes. Their eyes are milky white without pupils or irises.

"Their mouths are moving, and they seemed to be chanting something, but I can't understand them. I continue to climb the stairs, and now, looking up, I can see there's some sort of huge marble landing at the top. A throne of stone and gold stands in the middle of the landing and someone is sitting there.

"He's nude, and his skin is bronze but shot through with some sort of glimmering flecks. His face is hidden in a nimbus of light. All around me, the chanting of the shackled people is growing louder. I can make out the words, but I still can't understand them."

"Aenok Omo'nam!" The shackled people say. "Aenok Omo'nam!"

'Now the figure on the throne is holding up one of the iron collars. He's leaning over me. He says, "And now you will serve me here in paradise!"

Porter dropped the fabric and slumped back in his chair. Some of the D.A.'s people entered the frame and the video went black.

"What do you think?" Jack said from behind me. I turned my head and saw he was standing in the office doorway.

"He was living it as he saw it. Porter was the real deal."

Jack came in and sat back down. "I agree, but here's the thing. Anyone familiar with the Zodiac knows he claimed that the people he killed would serve him in the afterlife. He called it paradise, but misspelled it with a 'c' instead of an 's'."

I said, "Just like on the message at Porter's house."

"Yeah. All I'm saying is, Porter could have known about that in advance, though he said he didn't. There's something else."

Jack opened the file folder he'd just retrieved and flipped through some pages. He selected one page and handed it to me. It was a copy of one of the messages from the Zodiac. It read:

This is the Zodiac speaking. Have you cracked the last cipher I sent you? My name is_

And under that was printed what looked like:

A E N ☐ K ☐ M ☐ N A M

The 'letters' also included the Zodiac's symbol and a weird little mark apparently meant to separate omo from nam. Now my memory clicked into place.

I said, "I've heard the name Aenok before."

Jack leaned forward in his chair. "So it's a name."

"Yeah, the name of a demon."

Jack said, "That's the message the Zodiac sent after he killed Paul Stine. He also sent a blood-stained strip he'd torn from Stine's shirt. The same one Porter was given. Again, information Porter could have had from reading about the case, but I don't think so. I think he was literally seeing through Stine's eyes, right up to and right after the Zodiac shot him in the back of the head."

"So this time, the Zodiac's cipher wasn't actually a cipher," I said.

Jack said, "He was hiding the name in plain sight."

I said, "And it fits what I know about Aenok. The demon is mentioned in Egyptian and Mesopotamian texts, but he's far older than that. He's known as a soul eater. He collects the souls of the departed at the time of their deaths so he can torment them for eternity."

Jack said, "But the Zodiac said the victims would serve him, not this Aenok."

I said, "True, but it's possible the Zodiac had made a pact with Aenok. As the old saying goes, the dark gods grant boons for sacrifices."

Jack said, "But what did Porter see? The Zodiac was still alive at that point, so was that the afterlife?"

I said, "The being Porter saw may have been Aenok, or an avatar of the demon. Or maybe the Zodiac was existing on two planes at once. Time doesn't always work the same way on all levels of existence. It's also possible Aenok was inhabiting the killer's body, using his human form, and now he may be doing it again."

Jack said, "But why now. After all this time?"

I said, "My guess would be Porter. Even though he was seeing through Stine's eyes, he may have drawn Aenok's attention in that other realm. I think that's how he found Porter. The poor guy had established a link without knowing it. Keep in mind Jack, I'm speculating here. Things aren't usually as cut and dried as we'd like when dealing with demonic entities from any pantheon."

Jack leaned back in his chair and rubbed his eyes. "Jeez, I can't believe I'm sitting here discussing this stuff. So you really think the Zodiac and this demon thing have been hoarding the souls of all these people in a kind of private heaven?"

"Heaven for the killer, hell for his prisoners. Yes, I think it's true. From what I've heard and read, soul eaters capture the departing spirit at the moment of death and keep it from moving on."

Jack said, "Christ. Is there any way we can help those people?"

"It would require finding the demon and destroying it. That's possible, but it would take some doing."

The phone on Jack's desk rang and he snatched it up. He said about three words, then hung up and turned back to me. "The detective in charge of Porter's murder wants a meeting. Feel like riding over to police headquarters?"

"Yeah, I'd like to see what they're doing on the case."

"Spinning their wheels, probably. Maybe this new Zodiac will send us a letter or cipher. There are things forensics can do now with physical evidence they couldn't do 50 years ago."

I said, "If it is a copycat. We don't know for certain the Zodiac is dead. He may have yet to reach the paradise Aenok is preparing for him."

"Come on, Gavin. The guy would have to be in his eighties."

"We aren't dealing with a normal killer here," I said.

We left the office and took the elevator down to the street. Like at the airport, Jack had parked in a No Parking spot in front of the federal building.

He was turning his head to say something to me when his skull exploded.

A second later I heard the crack of a high-powered rifle and I went to the ground, scrambling for cover behind Jack's car. As near as I could tell, the shots had come from the parking garage across the street.

I counted to ten, then jumped up and ran full out across the street. I heard another shot, but the bullet went wild, and then I was inside the garage. I paused for a moment behind a concrete support, then ran for the stairs. From the angle of the shot, I was pretty sure the shooter had fired from the top level.

I pounded up the stairs, taking then two at a time, only pausing before making a turn to the next level in case he was waiting for me. I was especially cautious when I reached the roof, but no one was up there and there were only a couple of cars. I could see under them from my vantage point looking out of the stairwell. The shooter was in the wind. I walked over to the edge of the roof. No brass and no other physical evidence I could see. Just a message, scrawled on the wall with black paint.

Golden Gate Avenue
Oct 1-24
By Gun
Aenok sees you.

From below I could hear the wail of sirens in the distance.

#   #   #

An hour later I was sitting in the office of FBI Assistant Director Neal Durham. Durham looked more like and accountant than a G-Man. I had watched the EMTs load Jack's body into an ambulance and given my statement three times to three different policemen. Then the FBI scooped me up. I'd told Durham everything I thought he needed to know since Jack picked me up at the airport.

"I'm really sorry about Jack, Mr. Lee," Durham said, when my debriefing was finished. "He was a fine agent. Well-liked and well respected."

I said, "He was all that, for sure."

Durham said, "I'm not sure what to tell you now. Do you plan to stay in San Francisco?"

What he was saying was 'We real FBI agents don't need your ooky-spooky stuff, so your participation in the investigation is pretty much done'. I got it. He hadn't seen the things Jack had.

I said, "I'll be here a bit longer."

"Ah. Give me your phone number and I'll make sure you're kept informed on our progress. I want to assure you we'll be doubling down on our search for the killer. This entire field office is being mobilized as we speak."

I stood up. "You won't have to find him."

"What do you mean?"

I just smiled and walked out.

#   #   #

I waited until well after dark before looking for what I needed. I wanted a big, enclosed open space, with a lot of room to maneuver. I broke into a warehouse near the Embarcadero and disabled its security system. I'd stopped at a hardware store and a grocery store earlier to pick up the other things I'd be using.

I started by driving a steel peg into the concrete floor. I'd apologize to the warehouse owner later. I attached a long piece of cord and used that to draw a big circle on the floor with a chunk of blue chalk. Then I let the cord out a bit more drew a second circle about one foot wider than the first.

I lit some candles and put them in the proper positions, and then I began chalking a set of runes in the space between the two circles. Once in a while I'd stop and recite an incantation. I'm not the best at that sort of thing, but it was something I'd used several times before.

I'd told Jack it would take some doing to find the demon and destroy it, and that was true. So I would make it find me. What I was doing now was a bad idea by every definition of the word bad. And I could only do it because I had the Demon's name. But if I didn't do it, the authorities might never catch the new Zodiac and while they were trying, more people would die and have their souls stolen.

It took me about an hour to finish marking the circle. That was the first part of my plan. I blew out the candles and sat down on the floor to wait.

About another hour passed before I heard someone at the side door where I'd broken in. It was possible it was a security guard, of course, but I didn't think so. I head the door open, and I could just make out a figure against the dim light cast by a streetlamp. He came into the warehouse and walked across the floor. He had something in his hand. I was pretty sure it was a gun.

When the figure was halfway across my circle I made one final mark in the runes. Then I stood up and turned on the lights. A man wearing a dark jacket and a black ballcap stood in the circle. He squinted when the lights came on and leveled a semiautomatic pistol at me. He smiled.

"I'm not sure how you made me come here," the guy said. "But you should have come armed."

I smiled. "I didn't make you come here. Your patron demon did that. I used a low level summoning spell. Aenok could ignore it, but I figured that you, as his avatar couldn't."

Ballcap got a funny expression on his face. "What do you mean?"

"He's working through you. You're part of him now, but not a part that matters."

"We'll see who matters when you're my slave in…"

"Yeah, yeah. Paradise with a 'c'. Heard it before. Not going to happen. The first Zodiac is there, but you won't be joining him, and he's about to get evicted."

"Evict this, fuck head," Ballcap said, and pulled the trigger.

The bullet left the gun, ran out of energy almost immediately, and struck the invisible barrier of the inner circle before falling to the floor. Ballcap fired twice more with the same result.

I said, "You're standing in a summoning circle, used to bring demons from any number of different planes of reality. It's designed to contain energies spawned in Hell and worse places. Your handgun doesn't even register. You were good enough to walk into it and I sealed it."

"You're some kind of sorcerer?" Ballcap said.

I shook my head. "I just know a few tricks. I've killed demons and their familiars before.

I heard a truck rumble by and reminded myself I needed to get this over with. The worst part was coming and I had one ugly task left to get me there.

I said, "Mind telling me how you got involved with Aenok? I'd like to know what makes someone do something like that."

He grinned. "He came to me. Aenok, Lord of All, sought me out. Me. I'd been studying the Zodiac murders for years. I believed what he said about paradise, and I wanted that too."

"But you hadn't killed anyone?"

"I hadn't worked up to it. But Aenok came to me and gave me the strength to be like his other avatar."

I said, "And you enjoyed it?"

His grin grew wider and he actually licked his lips. "More than I ever imagined. The power over life and death is the power of the gods."

"Or some sad shlub with a gun," I said. "But thanks. It makes what I have to do a little easier."

"You're going to kill me, aren't you?"

"Not directly," I said. "Aenok will do that when he comes."

"Aenok would never harm me. I am his champion. His paladin."

I said, "You're his tool and nothing more. Just like your predecessor, a way to gather souls. Oh, he'll spare you a few as he did with the Zodiac, but that's all."

I stepped up to the circle and began to relight the candles. Ballcap ran up to the invisible barrier and watched me. He had a big knife in his hand. Maybe he thought he'd have better luck stabbing me than shooting me. He didn't.

"What are you doing?" he said.

I said, "Now I'm using a high-level spell of demon summoning. Aenok won't be able to resist this one. Unfortunately for you, in order to be sure, I have to use you as a conduit. He'll be coming through you."

I stepped back and began to the invocation. The overhead lights flickered, and the atmosphere became heavy. Ballcap looked all around as if expecting to see Aenok at any moment. He didn't get to see him. But he felt him.

I heard the sounds of bones breaking and then Ballcap began to scream as his skin split and blood splattered everywhere. His body was torn in two as something climbed out of it. Something that grew as it emerged, rising to about eight feet. It was roughly humanoid, with digitigrade legs like a saurian, but the arms and torso of a man. Its head was mostly jaws and teeth, with tiny red eyes set in deep sockets.

When it spoke, its voice was a deep, grating whisper which I heard both with my ears and inside my head. "You. Who are you to call me to this plane?"

I said, "I know your true name, so I'll give you mine. I'm Gawain, a knight of Camelot."

Aenok took a step forward and encountered the barrier. "You are not very brave for a knight. Release me and I'll tear you to bloody bits and devour your soul."

I said, "Answer a question first. Why did you take notice of this world again? You've been gone for years."

"One of you looked into my realm. I followed his thoughts back. I had completely forgotten this pitiful stain on reality. I've been reaping souls elsewhere. But now, I plan to take many more from here because of the intrusion on my domain."

Porter. I'd been right, then. I started walking around the circle, putting some distance between Aenok and me.

I said, "I suspected as much. I won't let you do that."

Aenok laughed. The laughter of demons is not a pleasant sound. "Release me, and you can try and stop me."

I said, "No, I don't think letting you out is a good idea. Tell you what. I'll come in there."

I stepped inside the circle.

Inside I could smell the raw animal stink of the demon and hear it breathing. The red eyes glittered and it opened and closed its claws in anticipation. I figured Aenok weighed about 600 pounds, so almost three times my weight. That was okay. I didn't plan on wrestling it. I opened my hand and my sword appeared in it.

Aenok cocked its head like a confused hound. "A magic weapon? You really are a knight. It won't help you. After I pull your limbs and head off you'll be my thrall."

I didn't say anything. I couldn't let it distract me. Aenok was a major demon, and while not in the class of say, Asmodeus, he was still an incredibly powerful entity. If I wasn't very careful he would kill me.

The demon took my silence as fear and charged. It was like standing in front of an oncoming bus. I waited until the last possible moment, then dodged to one side, cutting at Aenok's leg as it passed me. I cut deep and the demon shrieked. But it also struck out and its clawed hand raked across my shoulder.

I felt like I'd been hit by a car, and I fell hard on the unforgiving concrete. I kept rolling as I hit, which is all that kept Aenok from stomping me to death. I managed to get to my feet and bring up the sword in time to keep the demon from grabbing me. I ripped upwards with the blade and two of its fingers went flying.

Aenok was limping but I was pretty sure my shoulder was dislocated. That's not good for sword fighting. I circled to the demon's left. It turned with me, keeping its eyes fixed on my sword. It knew the weapon could hurt it now.

That's when I backed into the remains of Ballcap's body and fell over backwards. I released the sword as I hit, and it vanished. If I let it go it returns to where it came from. Aenok roared in triumph and charged at me as fast as its injured leg would let it. I could feel the ground shake as the demon hurtled my way.

I wasn't going to be able to get to my feet in time to recall the sword and mount any sort of defense against such a massive opponent, so I didn't try. I simply rolled out of the circle. It wasn't designed to keep me in. Aenok had forgotten the invisible wall and slammed into it at full charging speed. Even a demon is affected by that kind of impact. Aenok bounced off the wall and went down.

I was already in motion, and I leaped back into the circle. The sword appeared in my hand and as Aenok tried to rise I put everything into my swing and cut off its head. Thick black blood spurted like a fountain and the demon's body flopped about for a few seconds before Aenok finally lay still.

I staggered out of the circle and rubbed some of the chalk away with my foot. The barrier was gone. Aenok's body was already beginning to disintegrate. The demon wasn't part of this world and the matter he was composed of wouldn't remain now that it was no longer animate.

The floor was a mess though, between Ballcap's bloody remains and the chalk. That was regrettable but I couldn't hang around to straighten up. I gathered my stuff and got out of there.

I didn't stay in town for Jack's funeral. I've been to too many of those. I didn't tell Durham he wouldn't be finding his killer. What would be the point, since I couldn't really explain why. The cops might wonder about the mess in the warehouse but there was nothing to link it to the Zodiac killings, new or old.

The destruction of Aenok would undo everything done with the demon's power. The Zodiac's Paradise was no more, and the souls of all his servants and any others Aenok had collected were free. That had been worth the risk, and I hoped Jack would have thought it worth his life. Of course, since he was killed by one of Aenok's avatars, he would have gone to that other realm like Porter, Stine, and the others. I like to think that when 'Paradice' evaporated, Jack knew it was me that had been responsible. Cold comfort, but all I have.

GHOST FLIGHT

By Dennis K. Crosby

FOR THE MOMENT, UMAR TAN was not looking over his shoulder. He wasn't second-guessing every activity around him or the intent of others in his path. His heart wasn't racing at the slightest noise. His breathing was steady. There were no sweaty palms. He actually felt like he might even be able to sleep.

Soundly.

Peacefully.

Gratefully.

<Attention passengers, if you could please take your seats to let all passengers board and stow their luggage, we'll be able to push back and take off on time to your destination. Thank you.>

The flight attendant was pleasant. The entire crew, in fact, seemed pleasant. That was also a factor in his mood. Everything seemed to be going right.

I beat it! I won!

A smile betrayed his thoughts. But why shouldn't he be happy? Twelve months ago, he was anything but. Twelve months ago, his world was shattered. A chance encounter with someone, some… thing… helped him put the pieces back together. Now, he had everything he needed. Money.

Freedom. And Farah.

He felt her hand in his and gave it a gentle squeeze. The warmth filled his soul. A tingle of electricity traveled through his body. He felt her head rest on his shoulder, and he joined her in the loving gesture. They were about to start a new life, in a new country. Where they could be together in public. Where he could love her openly. Where they could thrive, have children, and grow old together as they were meant to. As they'd planned to.

Before the accident.

Before she'd died.

\#   \#   \#

"And stay out!"

The words echoed throughout the alleyway as Umar Tan landed headfirst in a muddy patch behind Jian's Pub. Only, it was not mud. It was the worst possible alternative.

Tonight was the third time in the past week, and the fifteenth week of the last twenty that he'd been kicked out. It was, however, the first time that he'd been told he could not return. He got to his feet, but unsteady legs set him back down. He reached for a random piece of newspaper to try and wipe himself clean, and he promptly toppled over.

He briefly thought of Farah and how ashamed she would be. For the first few weeks following her accident, he'd mourned respectfully, and in a way that did not embarrass her memory, or legacy in the village they'd been born to and grew up in. Her family had been appreciative of that and supported him—as did his own. But not long after she'd been laid to rest, after he'd returned to their home in Kuala Lumpur, something changed. No one knew what it was that had caused the shift. Umar had kept that to himself. It was enough though for him to enter into an abusive relationship with alcohol.

Where most would feel embarrassment at being shunned by those who'd once been friends, Umar felt nothing. There was a void where pride should be. In place of self-respect was a chasm lined with loneliness and pieces of his broken heart and spirit. It is said that when someone you love dies, a part of you dies, too. For Umar Tan, no truer words had ever been spoken. But more than a *part* of him died with Farah. She was everything to him. Had been for as long as he or anyone else could remember.

He attempted to get up again. He was weak, though, from both drinking and self-loathing. He made it to his hands and knees and crawled toward the next building, hoping to use its strength to stand. As he closed in, his vision narrowed, and he collapsed. In the distance, he heard voices. The volume increasing with each passing moment.

"Hmmmm," he moaned. An attempt at asking for help.

"What the…?" said a deep voice.

"Is that…Tan?" said a second voice.

Umar heard laughter.

He heard taunting.

Then he felt the poking and the kicking.

He felt no physical pain from the assault. It was unlikely that he'd feel it in the morning either, as the weight of being hungover usually blocked all other sensations. He'd been in this position before. No shame. No care. No… nothing. Secretly, he hoped the kicking wouldn't stop. He wanted them to continue until they'd ended his life. Maybe in death he would find happiness again—with Farah.

As he braced for another blow, he heard what sounded like a low growl. A dog maybe? His attackers murmured something. And then they screamed. In unison. In terror. In agony. The sound of tearing and ripping carried through the night air. The splash of liquids on the ground and against the walls left him curious—as much as he could be in his current state. Umar wondered if death had finally come to claim him.

He rolled onto his back, content to let the growling terror take him. Instead, he felt himself being lifted. That growl he'd previously heard was now replaced with light purring. It was the only way to describe it. He was being carried gently. He felt warmth and wondered if this was what Farah had felt in her last moments. In a short time, he felt himself lowered to something soft. He did not move. Something covered him. It was warm.

Death was here.

Finally.

"Rest, Umar Tan," said a gentle voice.

The soft purring continued, and before long, dizzying darkness came.

\#   \#   \#

The following morning Umar awoke in his own bed. On fresh sheets. In clean sleepwear. It was raining, but that was nothing new. Everything else aside, Umar had only one question.

"Am I dead?" he whispered.

Searching his memory, he recalled being out the night before and drinking to excess, as had been his normal practice of late. He vaguely recalled being kicked out of the pub, but that memory was also so common that it could have come from any number of nights over the past several months. The sensation of being abused, along with echoes of growls and purrs, though? Those were new memories.

Umar got up from bed, slid into house shoes, and walked toward his kitchen. He heard light clanking and movement. More curious than fearful—after all, he'd made his peace with death and was ready for it—he continued. Umar rounded the corner and was hit with a sudden jolt. His heart skipped. Umar grabbed his chest. His legs lost strength. He went to his knees. With blurred vision he watched his wife run to his aid.

"My love! Are you okay? What is it? What's wrong?" she asked.

Speechless, he reached out and caressed her face. She was real. Her flesh was warm. There was color in her cheeks. Her hazel eyes sparkled as they always had. Her lips were curled with concern.

"You're...here," he said weakly.

"Yes. Yes of course. Where else would I be?"

"Am I...dead?" he asked, confused.

"What? No! Of course not," said Farah with a light chuckle. "Did you have a bad dream?"

"I...I..."

He couldn't find the words. He couldn't take his eyes off her, either. He felt a smile form. He felt a tear fall. Then he felt her in his arms.

"Oh, my love," began Farah, "I am worried about you."

She held him tightly. After a few moments, she helped him to his feet and guided him to a chair at the kitchen table. Umar landed heavily as the weight of grief, shock, confusion, and love sat with him.

"You work so hard," she said, walking away from him. "Here…eat."

Farah returned to him with a small plate. Two soft-boiled eggs and two pieces of Kaya toast. Umar looked from her to the plate and back again… still astonished. She walked away to retrieve coffee and sweet coconut jam with butter.

"Kaya jam?" asked Umar.

Farah nodded.

Still confused, but surprisingly hungry, Umar spread the jam on his toast and took a bite. He chewed for several seconds before he realized there was nothing there. He looked in his hand and found the toast there, still complete. He took a bite again, chewed, and again…nothing.

"My love…eat," said Farah.

Umar turned his attention to her, saw her smile, and then…watched as skin and hair gave way to ash. Finally, whisps of gray smoke replaced her. Those same whisps replaced his toast, and his plate…and his coffee. All that was left was the sound of rain tap dancing on the roof of his home. In the sink, the same dishes that had been there for two weeks. Pockets of dirt, dust, and what may have been water were on the floor. Defeated, Umar lowered the hand that once held his breakfast and let it fall to his lap. He then saw that he was fully clothed—in the same soiled garments from the night before.

A light purr floated through the air.

"Would you like it to be real next time?" asked a voice from behind.

Umar jumped up and ran to the counter. He grabbed anything he could find to serve as a weapon. Securing a knife, he turned. A hooded figure stood in the kitchen doorway. Beneath the drops of rain, he heard the growl and saw a flash of red beneath the hood. After a few short moments, the purring returned.

"Do not be afraid," said the figure. "I am…a friend."

The purring continued, and it took some time for Umar to realize that the sound was emanating from the hooded man. Umar was a man a science, of mathematics. For everything, there was a logical explanation. This? This was something vastly different. Very…impossible. Maybe he was dreaming.

Maybe he was still drunk.

Maybe he actually *was* dead.

"Wh…what…are you?"

"Dig deep. I think you already know."

The devil? Death itself? Despite the stranger's claims Umar did not know. None of this made sense.

"If you are here to take me away, then do it. I have nothing left."

"It's all right, Umar. You are safe. I promise. I'm not here to take you anywhere. In fact, it was I who brought you home last night," said the hooded man.

Umar's eyes widened. Shaking, Umar felt more tears fall. Neither the shaking, nor the tears were the result of fear, though. They were the result of realizing that Farah had not been there at all. His…waking dream had been just that. A dream.

"What did you do to me?!"

"I found you last night. I chased away your attackers and brought you home. You spoke a lot, most of it incoherent. But the one name that came through clearly…was Farah. When I asked about her, you said she was your wife. I asked if you missed her, and you said yes. I asked if you wanted her back…and you said yes. So, this morning, I gave her back to you."

"How? Wh…wh…why? Why would you do that? Why would you give her back to me, only to take her away?"

"I…thought it would be a way to help your grief. It is strong. Powerful. And that is extremely dangerous for you, my friend. I hoped that one last moment with her, one last sweet morning, would be helpful."

Umar stood, stunned. His knife hand shook. Tears streamed. His face contorted. Then he screamed. In that scream was the pain he'd felt for weeks on end. He dropped the knife and ran at the stranger. Umar threw punches. His fists repeatedly pounded on the stranger's chest.

"I understand this pain. I invite you to let it out," said the stranger, unmoved.

"Bring her back!" Umar screamed.

The stranger grasped Umar's arms tightly. Umar still could not make out the man's face, but his strength was otherworldly. He tried to wrestle his arms free, but there was no hope. Finally, he let his arms go limp and after several seconds, the hooded man released his grip.

"Who are you?" asked Umar, backing up slowly.

The stranger pulled back his hood and Umar gasped.

For decades, he'd heard stories of a being, a ghost, a spirit in Malaysian mythos with immense power—Hantu Raya. From his father, his grandmother, and a host of cousins, uncles, and aunts he learned that Hantu Raya was a spirit with the power to bestow anything to its master. It was a changeling, able to become anyone or anything it chose. It also served as a protector to its master, not unlike the Jinn of Middle Eastern lore. Some even said that Hantu Raya could use its power to shift reality if that was what its master required. There were drawings of the spirit. Sometimes with horns. Sometimes with red eyes and yellowed canines. Even fangs and a long hairy tail. No one really knew what its natural form was. According to lore, to see its true form meant you were marked for death. But while its appearance was undetermined, there was shared belief in how one would know they were in the presence of the spirit.

"You will know Hantu Raya, because as a sign of respect and fealty, it will take your form," said Umar's father.

For decades he'd chalked it up to Malaysian superstition. Flights of fancy from generations long gone. Yet, in his kitchen, Umar Tan stared at himself. A perfect duplicate. Right down to the small scar on his left cheek.

"You are the spirit," began Umar, "Hantu Raya."

"I am," said the spirit with a nod.

"Why are you here?"

"I heard your cries. Not just last night, but for weeks on end. Your pain called to me, and I wanted to help."

"At what cost?" asked Umar.

Everything in life came at a cost. Of that, Umar was certain.

"No cost," said the spirit. "I hoped this would be a gift. A way for you to see that, even though she is gone, her loving memory remains. And that, in itself, is a gift that few humans get."

Umar looked from the spirit to the table where he'd been sitting. He replayed the scene he thought had been real. In his mind Farah kissed him.

She handed him breakfast, coffee, and jam. She sat with him. This time though, she didn't fade away. They continued to talk in this vision. They laughed. In the end, she turned her head and looked at him, the *real* him, and held out a hand.

She faded when he reached for her.

His eyes misted.

His heart ached.

"Can you make it real? Can you bring her back for good?" asked Umar.

Umar saw hesitation in the spirit. The answer was clear. He could do it. He could bring Farah back. The prospect filled Umar with excitement. In an instant, his fortunes, his very life, could change.

"It is within my power to do that, yes," said the spirit. "But then there *would* be a great cost. For both of you. I don't think that's something you would be prepared for."

"That's not true. I would. Please, bring her back to me. I'll do anything!"

"You don't know what that means."

"Then tell me!" demanded Umar. "Please..."

Even Umar could hear the desperation in his voice. Would it be enough to persuade the spirit to help him?

"The cost would be sacrifice, Umar Tan. Two, to be exact. You would offer a regular sacrifice to me, of your choosing, but one that could sustain me."

"And the other," said Umar, eagerly.

"The other," began the spirit, "Is harder. As a spirit of this land, I am bound to it. If I am bound to it, so too are those whom I protect. If I brought your wife back, you would be bound to this land for the rest of your days."

"That would be—"

"And," said the spirit, cutting him off. "No one could ever know she was alive."

"But...she will be...like a prisoner," said Umar.

"No one. Can. Know," said the spirit emphatically.

Umar contemplated what life would be like under the conditions outlined. In the big scheme of things, they were not terrible. Life without Farah was unbearable. It was, in fact, no life at all. But to keep her hidden?

Could he do that? Could she?

After several moments of contemplation, Umar said softly, "I…cannot do that to her."

He hated himself. Happiness and joy were within reach, and he was walking away from it. It was the right thing to do, though. Wasn't it? Bringing her back was so unnatural to begin with. Would she even be herself? Would it feel the way it did when he'd thought she was there making breakfast? The temptation was there. Still, saying no was the right thing to do.

Right?

"Very well, Umar Tan," said the spirit. "For what it's worth, I believe you've made the right choice. The balance between life and death is delicate. Upsetting that has…consequences. For everyone. I respect your decision and wish you well."

The spirit placed a hand on its chest, a symbol of respect. It turned to leave, then stopped, and shared a warning with Umar.

"Your grief is heavy. It's like a beacon to all manner of spirit and demon. It was powerful enough to call me, and that is no easy feat, so rest assured it *will* call others. Not all of them will be so…kind. Should you need my help, just ask. I'm never too far."

Umar nodded.

"Home is where the heart is, Umar Tan," said the spirit. "You will never fully be at peace, or feel at home, until your heart is mended. I am happy to help, but I cannot help you if you are dead."

Umar nodded again.

The spirit walked away. As it exited the front door, Umar was caught by the sound of the purring. It was calm. Peaceful. The spirit slowly faded with each step it took away from the home, until it was completely gone from sight.

#   #   #

As the passengers continued to board, Umar took notice of a young girl walking behind her father. She couldn't have been more than five, maybe six, and she clutched a white teddy bear close to her chest. He smiled at her. She smiled back. He dared to wonder what his own daughter would look like one day. What toys would she hold dear?

"What is your bear's name?" asked Umar.

Shyly, the girl held the bear closer to her chest and giggled.

"Go on. Tell him," said the girl's father.

"His name is Umar," she said.

"What? Really?" gasped Umar, genuinely surprised. "That's my name, too."

Umar and the girl laughed together.

"He must be the smartest, kindest bear in the world, then," said Umar.

"He is."

The little girl giggled again.

"Well, you be sure and take care of him, and he will take care of you."

In an instant, the girl's nervous laughter ceased. She grew sad. Tears streamed down her face. She closed her eyes tightly to try and stop them. Confused, Umar reached out to try and comfort her, to apologize for anything he'd said wrong.

He stopped short when she opened her eyes again.

The once brown orbs were now bright red. They pulsed in rhythm with his heartbeat which was slowly increasing. The little girl's grin widened unnaturally, revealing sharp teeth and a forked tongue. He heard a low growl that vibrated through the cabin floor to his seat. The once white teddy bear was now streaked with stains of blood. The center of the stuffed animal burst open and long black tendrils flew out, grabbing Umar's arms and head. With a firm grip, they began to pull him toward the dark abyss in the bear's chest.

"You cannot escape, Umar Tan," said the girl in a low gravelly voice.

Umar flailed about wildly, desperate for freedom.

He fought.

He screamed.

He woke up.

"Umar! Umar!" said Farah, desperate concern in her voice.

"Sir, are you okay?" asked another.

Umar looked up. He found Farah to his left in her seat. To his right, a flight attendant. Both were nervous. His breathing was rapid. He grabbed at his chest, tried to catch his bearings, then sat back, head rested against his seat.

A dream?

"I...I...I'm fine," he said between breaths. "I must have dozed off. We travelled a long way, with little sleep. I guess I was more tired than I realized."

Farah caressed his face, then his arm. She put her hand over his.

"Let me get you some water, sir," said the flight attendant.

"Yes, thank you."

"What happened? What did you dream? Was it...?"

"It was...the spirit. It had come for me."

Umar felt Farah tense up. She grasped his arm and held it tightly. He felt her head push against him.

"It won't come for you," she said.

"No. Of course not. It was just so...real."

It took several more moments for Umar to fully calm down. The flight attendant returned with a bottle of water and said she may have something stronger for him once they reached cruising altitude. They shared a smile. Farah laughed. People continued to board.

An elderly woman walked past him. Behind her, a man, presumably her husband, looked on and smiled. Umar felt the love between the strangers and again dared to imagine his life in the future with Farah. Away from this place. From the memories. From the darkness.

As he settled back into his seat, now calm, he saw a man with child's backpack walk toward him. Behind that man, was an adorable little girl, with a long ponytail and the biggest brown eyes, holding a white teddy bear close to her chest.

"Hold little Umar tightly so you don't drop him. Okay, sweetie?" said the father.

"Yes, papa," said the girl.

#   #   #

Word had gotten out about Umar's drunken antics. Again, it was

144

nothing new. But the intensity had elevated to an unprecedented level. So much so, that his employer let him go. They'd called it a leave of absence, but the writing was on the wall. He wouldn't be welcomed back. And the leave was without pay. Because of his years of service, they'd agreed to give him a generous severance package. Between that, and the insurance payout on Farah's death, he'd be okay for quite some time. At least, financially.

Umar returned home and packed some things, got into his car, and drove. The city would give him nothing he needed. Though, he didn't even know what he needed. No. That wasn't true.

He needed her.

He needed Farah.

After hours of travel, he arrived at his small home just outside the little village where Farah and Farah had grown up. He hadn't been back since her funeral service. This was as close as he was going to get to being with her again.

The words of Hantu Raya echoed in his mind. Enough to make him wonder…what if. What if he brought her back? They could live away from people, from prying eyes, from any and everyone. They could live the rest of their days together in peace.

"No," he whispered to himself. He still recognized that a life hiding, away from the world, was no life at all.

Umar unpacked, made some tea, then sat outside. The skies were cloudy, but the weather was otherwise calm and pleasant. A light breeze jostled the trees. Birds flew overhead. And for a moment, perhaps the first in a great many weeks, Umar Tan was at ease.

He hadn't realized how long he'd been outside. Before he knew it, the sun was setting. The puffy clouds absorbed the red orange colors of the sky making the heavens above look like they were on fire. And it was beautiful. He longed to share this with Farah again. He held back his tears, stood, and walked toward the house. Behind him, he heard a rustle and a whoosh of wind. He ignored it.

Until the wailing began.

Looking back, he spotted a shadow in the distance emerging from the wooded area. It had no form, but it moved swiftly, and with purpose. Umar was certain that the purpose was malice.

He rushed toward his door. The handle wouldn't turn. He gripped it tighter and tighter, twisted back and forth…and nothing. The wailing shadow increased in both sound and speed. Umar threw his whole body against the door. Nothing. Again and again, he tried, and it would not open. The shadow closed in. It grew as it bared down upon him. With one final massive thrust, Umar slammed into the door. Finally, it flew open. Falling inside, Umar scrambled to his feet to push the door shut. The shadow had reached the house, and it pushed back. Its wail was deafening. The power intense. Umar fought hard and finally managed to close the door firmly.

The shadow was not done. It banged against the door. It knocked repeatedly. It wailed incessantly. Until the morning came. Umar found peace. He didn't know what to make of it. He was, of course, scared. Terrified. What if it returned?

It did.

And it banged on the door and wailed.

Hour. After. Hour.

Night. After. Night.

After a week of this haunting, Umar tan finally gave in and spoke the words given to him by Hantu Raya.

"Help me."

#   #   #

<Ladies and gentlemen, we've closed the doors and will be preparing to push back shortly. At this time, we ask you to put away all electronic devices and turn your attention to our flight attendants as they share our safety information.>

As the flight attendants went through the motions, Umar felt a swirl of butterflies in his stomach. In just under six hours, he and Farah would be free. He finished the last of his water and wanted more, though the offer of "something stronger" was greatly appealing. Aside from an occasional glass of wine, Umar did not drink much alcohol anymore. Not like he did after Farah had died. Since her return, his life was…normal. As normal as one can get when you're hiding from the public and offering sacrifices to a benevolent spirit every week.

The way his life had changed. So swiftly. So drastically. It was unfathomable.

<We will, throughout taxi and takeoff, let you listen in as our pilot speaks to the tower. Now please sit back and enjoy this five-hour and thirty-four-minute flight to Beijing. Welcome aboard Malaysian Airlines flight three seventy.>

#   #   #

As he'd done every morning for almost twenty-two weeks, Umar Tan placed fresh flowers in a vase on the kitchen table, then set about making breakfast. And just as she'd done for the same amount of time, Farah, his wife, walked in and waited to be served. Umar sensed her as soon as she'd walked in. Her light steps did not betray her, but the scent of light jasmine did. This was how he started every day, and it was everything he could hope for.

He no longer regretted the pact he'd made with the spirit. Hantu Raya continued to explain the challenges that could arise, but Umar did not care. He wanted safety and protection from the dark spirits that prayed on his grief. And ultimately, he wanted his wife back. He wanted to be happy again. He knew it would be a tough road ahead, but it was one he was willing to traverse.

Thankfully, Farah was, too.

When she'd returned to him, he told her everything. It was the only way to prevent any potential break in his covenant with the spirit. Naturally, she was taken aback, but in the end, she agreed to do her part. She would remain hidden from the public. She would stay with her one true love until their last days. And they would never leave Malaysia. That was months ago. Things were going well. As was the morning routine.

Fresh flowers.

Breakfast.

A kiss from—

Wait! There was…no kiss.

Umar turned to see Farah sitting at the table. She looked at him and smiled, but there was no passion in the smile. It was…a chore. Was she unhappy? Had he done something? All of this seemed so uncomfortable, so cold, so…

"Are you well today?" he asked.

"Yes. I'm fine," said Farah.

"Are you sure?" followed Umar.

"Yes. Just…hungry," she said, smiling, and shifting in her chair.

Umar went back to prepare their morning meal. He served her plate when he was done, then made his own before sitting down with her.

"Do you like the flowers I picked today?" he asked. He'd asked that every morning. And every morning she'd fawned over their beauty and sweet fragrance.

"Yes. They are lovely," she said.

Lovely?

Umar watched as Farah moved food around on her plate. Her brief smile replaced by a flat affect that was neither happy nor sad…just…there.

"My love, what's wrong?" asked Umar, reaching out for her hand. Several seconds passed before she placed her hand in his. It took a lifetime before she spoke.

"Nothing," she said.

She gave his hand a squeeze, then quickly removed it and returned to moving food around her plate.

"Do you not like the food? I can make something different," he said.

"No. It's fine."

After she spoke, a petal fell from one of the flowers he'd picked. Umar watched as it slowly floated down, rocking back and forth, until it landed gently on the table. Even away from its fellow petals, it was beautiful. Singularly beautiful. Just as Farah was. There was also a sadness in its fall, as it likely signaled the pending death of the flower. The petal, now separated from its bunch, was already on the path to the afterlife.

Umar looked up at Farah. She too stared at the petal. Her gaze seemed less like recognizing its beauty, and more like connecting with it as a kindred spirit.

"The flowers are dying. They don't like being away from each other," she whispered.

"What better life though, than to be chosen, and loved by a few, or even one—than to just be among the many who are adored and loved," said Umar.

Umar saw a brief sparkle in Farah's eyes. But it was not joyful. Farah grabbed her fork and stabbed at her food. She ate swiftly. Furiously. And when her plate was clean, she got up from her chair, set it in the sink, and retreated to the bedroom.

Umar finished his meal in silence.

He cleaned the dishes in silence.

Then he left his home to offer his weekly sacrifice to the spirit.

When he returned home, though, and found it empty, the silence was replaced by his deafening scream.

"NOOOOOOOOOOO!"

#   #   #

After several hours of searching, Umar returned home, a bundle of nervous energy wrapped in a cloak of fear. Farah had gone. She was nowhere to be found. He even checked the village square. There was no sign of her. Surely if she'd been seen, there'd be much more frantic activity about the streets.

When he opened the door, exhausted, he found her sitting near the fireplace.

"Farah!"

Umar ran to her. He ignored his instinct to berate her and tell her what she'd done was foolish. Since breakfast, it was clear that she was unhappy, and that was not the state he wanted her in. That's not why he bargained with Hantu Raya for her return. He wanted to love her for the rest of his days. He wanted joyful nights with her in his arms.

A crackle in the fireplace echoed through the home.

Despite the warmth on his face, Umar found himself shaking. There were questions that needed to be asked, yet he was hesitant to pose them lest he drive her away again. There were two conditions for her return. He'd fulfilled one this morning. Had Farah, in her anger and despair, broken the other?

"I know why you did it, why you brought me back," said Farah. "And I am grateful to be loved so fully. But…"

But. That one word stopped his heart. Her next words could kill him. Umar prepared himself as best he could.

"…but what is a life with the one you love if you can't share it with the world?" she asked.

The words made him stand at attention. He knew them well. He'd spoken them at their wedding. In his haste to bring back the love of his life, he'd broken the most important covenant. The one he'd made on that special day.

"I'm…sorry," he said gently. "I did not fully anticipate this life…this new life…being so hard on you."

"I thought I could handle it," she said. "I thought, if I have you, things will be fine. But I just miss so much of the world."

It wasn't her words that got to him as much as her tears. Each one, a stab in his heart. What had he done?

"Perhaps…I don't know…I can…renegotiate," said Umar, starting to pace. He stopped and moved closer to her. "We have a covenant, but I am its master. It has protected us, and we've held up our end all these months. Maybe there's a way we can…"

For as long as they'd known each other, Umar and Farah had an uncanny ability to speak without speaking. Such was their bond. That ability served them now because the words she screamed with her eyes alone were deafening.

"Oh no. What did you do?" asked Umar.

"I…I…was angry. I felt confined. Lonely. I had—have—you, but there's so much out there. So many people."

She was repeating herself now. Another sign that something was very wrong.

"Did anyone see you?" asked Umar.

"We are human. We are social creatures. We can't be expected to never see anyone ever again."

"Did anyone see you?" asked Umar, slower this time.

"I was careful," said Farah.

Umar relaxed.

"But…I…on my way back, I felt…compelled. I had to see her. I knew how much my death hurt you. I could only imagine what it did to her. So, I had to see her. To ease her mind. To fill her heart with joy. I had to see my mother."

Umar's eyes widened.

"It's okay," said Farah, hurriedly. She was…surprised. Maybe a little frightened. Who wouldn't be? But in the end, she was simply happy to have me back as I knew she would be."

Umar started breathing heavily. Erratically. He felt his pulse rising.

"She won't say a word, my love. She swore," said Farah. "It's going to be okay. She's going to come here tonight and eat with us."

Umar shook his head.

"It's going to be okay. I promise," said Farah, repeatedly. Pleading her case.

"No," said Umar. "It won't be."

Farah just stared at Umar. Confusion. Hurt. Anger. All of them took space in her gaze.

"Farah, that was not your mother," said Umar.

"How dare you—"

"Your mother died two months after you did!"

He'd never told her. At the time he thought there'd be no point because they were forbidden to see anyone. Coming back from the dead was hard enough. It made no sense to add the burden of her mother's death to the shock of her own resurrection.

"No. That's…that's not possible. I saw her. It *was* her!"

It didn't take long for them to realize the truth. What she saw was not her mother. It could only have been one thing.

"It was…the spirit?" asked Farah, rhetorically.

The air shifted. Tension filled pockets around the room. There was no sound save the crackle of the fire. Outside, though, the skies darkened.

Flashes of lightning pulsed in the now gray-green clouds. Thunder rolled so heavily that the floor beneath them vibrated. The wind increased. The rustling of tree leaves spoke to the intensity. Umar clutched Farah in his arms. He knew what was coming.

"We need to leave here. Now!" screamed Umar.

"And go where?" asked Farah. "Where can we go where that thing won't find us?"

Umar had no answer. In all the legends, no one had ever bested a creature such as Hantu Raya. It was a spirit. It had no weaknesses. The only thing that would stop it from coming was…

"It's bound to the land," he said. "It cannot leave Malaysia. And it can only help us…or harm us, if we are alive."

"What? What are you saying?"

"Quickly, pack some clothes for us then wait for me in the car," said Umar quickly.

He ran through the house and out the back door to his outdoor workshop and retrieved two large cannisters of gasoline. As the storm picked up, he ran back to the house. He met Farah there and saw that she had two bags.

"Go," he said, gesturing toward the front door.

As Farah ran out, Umar set out to douse the floor and furniture liberally. Seconds later, he dropped a match and sprinted out the door.

#   #   #

<Three Seven Zero, three two right, cleared for take-off. Good night.>

<Three two right, cleared for take-off MAS Three Seven Zero. Thank you, bye.>

Umar heard the engines power up at the last exchange between the cockpit and the tower. The plane began to move. Faster. Faster. He bounced in his seat and held Farah's hand tightly. As the last wheels on the plane left the ground, he let out a sigh.

<Departure Malaysian Three Seven Zero.>

Umar felt Farah's hand on his knee.

"Stop that," she said.

He hadn't realized he'd been tapping his foot the entire time. The calm he'd felt when they'd first sat down was long gone. Likely the result of reliving the events that led them to their seats.

And that little girl.

"Do you really think we'll be safe?" she asked.

"Our house is gone. Even if the spirit realizes we did not die in the fire, we've bought ourselves enough time to get away. It once told me that my grief was so fierce that I'd called to it. With you here, I no longer grieve. It cannot hear what's not there. There will be no *one*, and no *thing*, looking for us."

"Then why are you nervous?"

"I…don't like to fly," said Umar.

It was several moments before they both burst out in nervous laughter. Umar Tan's job, before he was placed on a "leave of absence" was aeronautical engineer. In fact, he'd been responsible for the early designs of the very plane they were on. Some of that added to a sense of comfort.

<Malaysian Three Seven Zero, climb flight level three five zero.>

< Flight level three five zero, Malaysian Three Seven Zero.>

Umar kissed her forehead again and they both settled back as the plane continued to climb. Once they reached cruising altitude he glanced over his wife's head, out the window, and stared at the darkness and lights below. An occasional flash from the plane would illuminate the immediate area. In between flashes, a reflection in the window caught his eye.

It was the little girl.

He turned his head and found her standing next to him, clutching her white teddy bear. Nervously, he smiled at her, then said, "Do you need help finding your seat?"

She said nothing in return.

<Malaysian Three Seven Zero, maintaining level three five zero.>

Umar's smile disappeared. He sat up more, looking for help from someone, anyone. Deciding to take matters into his own hands, Umar unbuckled his seatbelt, stood, and said to the girl, "Come on. Let's go find your seat."

He walked with the young girl ahead of him. The lights were off in the cabin, though a few passengers had their overheads on for reading. After a few steps, those lights began to flicker. Seconds later, all the lights flickered. There was no pattern, but swiftly and intermittently, they turned on and off. Umar looked down to find that the girl had vanished. Ahead, and to the left of him, he saw her, nestled in her seat, fast asleep next to her father.

"Wh…wh…what?" he whispered.

Umar heard a low growl.

Turning his attention to the center of the aisle, he saw a dark, cloaked figure before him. Bright red eyes flashed. The figure pulled back its cloak to reveal its face…*his* face. Umar Tan was once again face-to-face with Hantu Raya.

"Did you really think you could escape me?" asked the spirit.

"No! Please! Take me if you must but spare my wife," Umar pleaded.

The low growl from the spirit reverberated in Umar's mind. Grabbing his head with both hands he tried to shut it out but there was no escape.

"You have broken the covenant," bellowed the spirit, drool dripping from its rancid mouth.

Umar turned to run. But there was nowhere to go. No place to hide. He looked around at the other passengers for help, but they were all asleep. Or had he killed them?

"Farah!" he screamed.

Umar ran back to his seat and found Farah sitting there, her head against the window. She looked lovely. Heavenly. For a moment he dared to wonder if that was where they'd end up. The loud growl and the now flashing red lights in the cabin were harbingers of anything but an afterlife of peace with his beloved.

"I'm…so…sorry," said Umar.

He looked back at Hantu Raya. The spirit took slow steps forward, then, in the blink of an eye, stood directly in front of Umar. The spirit grabbed him by the neck and lifted him off the cabin floor. Umar struggled to get loose, but his efforts were futile.

The lights went off.

When they came back on, Umar was standing on the cabin floor alone. The spirit was nowhere in sight. He looked over to Farah. Her eyes had opened. She sat up, expressionless, staring at him.

The lights went off again.

When they came back on, every passenger was now awake. Eyes wide. Expressionless. Staring at Umar.

Once again it went dark.

Low growls began. A wave of them. A flash of lightning outside illuminated the cabin briefly and Umar saw every passenger standing. This time, though, when the cabin went dark, it wasn't completely black. Instead, Umar saw an ocean of pulsing red eyes.

And the growling grew louder.

Deeper.

Umar was frozen. This was the end. Death was coming.

In the back of the plane, amid the glowing red eyes of the passengers and crew, Umar saw the spirit. It laughed, then its body contorted. Bones cracked. Ligaments popped. Skin ripped away. Muscles and tendons stretched. It grew in height. With a skeletal wiry frame, its arms flailed about. The cloak it wore gave way to ashen leathery skin. Umar couldn't speak. Fear had overtaken him.

Hantu Raya revealed its true form.

Static cut in overhead and the cabin was filled with sounds from the cockpit. Umar's eyes remained locked on the malevolent spirit as the captain spoke with the tower somewhere on the ground below.

<Malaysian Three Seven Zero, contact Ho Chi Minh one two zero decimal nine. Good night.>

<Good night. Malaysian Three Seven Zero.>

They would be out of Malaysian airspace soon. If he could just hold on a little longer, they would be safe. The spirit would be gone.

And then he felt it. Umar Tan felt the plane turn. As it did, Hantu Raya rushed down the aisle, a dark formless blur of terror. Umar screamed, shielding his face in some futile effort to protect himself.

A bright light flashed.

A loud piercing wail filled the cabin.

And then, Umar Tan and every soul aboard… vanished.

SENTIENT SLIME – EINSTEIN'S STOLEN BRAIN

By Melanie Schubert

THOMAS SIGHS AND DROPS THE bloodied scalpel into a metal dish with all the others. Not a weary sigh. More a breathless rattle of excitement—a rare sound that this green-tiled room that reeks of bleach has never heard in all its time. After all, excitement isn't something one comes upon often as a pathologist. Certainly not on any regular day conducting the autopsies of the dead.

But today is not regular. Neither is the body of the man laid out on the table before him.

Albert Einstein. Great genius of our time.

Time of death, 1:15am, April 18, 1955.

Cause of death: abdominal aortic aneurysm.

A ghost of a smile curls Thomas' lips. He doesn't mean to smile but he can't help it. It seems like awfully good luck he was called upon tonight.

No, not luck. Divine providence. He thinks.

That curls the smile right back to where it came from. He closes his eyes to drink in the energy of the moment. A small, solemn nod wags his head up and down. This was supposed to happen tonight, he realises. He's always been destined for greatness, and now, here it is, flesh yielding right under his own sharpened scalpel.

It's terrible of course—Einstein dying and all.

"But we all have to die at some point, don't we?" Thomas chuckles.

His eyes flit to the door as if suddenly remembering himself. He dabs his forehead and upper lip to catch the sweat beading there. He's grateful the nurse helping earlier went home so no one can judge what his face is doing. He frowns at the troubled looks he pictures clouding peoples' faces if they saw. *They have no right to judge him. It's perfectly understandable to feel this rush over such a celebrity. Only natural he should experience elation sifting through the gizzards of a god of our time*, Thomas thinks.

The cause of death is already confirmed, but Thomas can't bring himself to leave this room. The air feels full. The very room vibrates with the energy of Einstein even postmortem. Thomas' heart hasn't stopped racing. He can't remember it thrumming so fast. Not even when he'd felt the welcome wet of a woman for the first time. That was a rush, yes. But this is something else. Dizzying. Exhilarating. A feeling not of this world.

He wonders what could make a man able to command such a presence in death. He wants to know…

*No…*it's nothing so petty as a want.

He *needs* to know.

Knows it will consume his every waking breath.

It is the moment Thomas has waited for all his life. His chance to drink from the chalice of the greats and rise up into his own power.

His eyes creep back over to Einstein's head. To the white, iconic fluff that crowns it.

It's all there, locked behind a thin sheet of skull. The brain that redetermined the laws of physics. Gave us the laws of relativity. A mind beyond any human of our time.

Thomas takes quick bouncing steps around the room as he thinks and mutters. "Man's a genius. Spectacular. Spectacular man's got to have a spectacular brain. It's all in there. All the secrets. The power."

He shakes his head. Another chuckle escapes his lips. "Well, we can't very well just shove it in the earth—and besides, they didn't say *not* to remove the brain, now did they?"

He doesn't waste any more time arguing with himself. It's divine providence, divine reason. He will not question it any longer. Thomas picks up his saw.

He pauses to offer a prayer of gratitude. He isn't sure if his prayer is to god, or Einstein. If he were honest, he isn't particularly concerned with the wishes of either right now. But uttering the words makes the moment feel blessed and profound.

The saw feels light as its teeth meet flesh. The skull is harder to get through. Sweat drips as he saws. Thomas hums a few bars of *That's Amore* as he works. It's running on full blast in his head.

He frowns and shakes his head. *No that won't do.* He can't be singing about the moon and pizza pies in the presence of genius. He should probably be humming a sonata. But Thomas doesn't know any sonatas. He scowls at himself and this failure and stops humming, just as the final bit of bone is sawn loose.

There's a hiss of air then a pop. Like the hiss of an alley cat giving warning and the pop of a cap gun. Thomas pauses, hands trembling with holy reverence. Then another chuckle slides out. Because of course Einstein's head would hiss. That feels perfectly right. The master must protect his magnum opus. But not from him. The skull has already yielded beneath his saw. It is ready for him. Wants him to see.

Oh, he'll see soon enough…

Thomas pauses, runs his fingers along the cut in wonder. A shining gold excretion bleeds thickly out the edges where skin has torn like paper away from bone. In all his years conducting autopsies, Thomas has never seen anything like it. His heart is in raptures. For here it is; a holy sign this moment has been preordained by a power greater than any could ever imagine.

He rubs the slick, viscous fluid between his fingers. He doesn't remember when his gloves came off, but he can't deny wanting to feel the texture of the excretion himself.

He will feel it in every cell of marrow in his bones…

It manages to feel both light, and dense. Solid one moment, supple and yielding the next. As more drips out it takes on other colors. Greys and sulfurous yellows, that bring to mind the shades of certain lichen, textured with flat bubbles like lanced boils.

Thomas' eyes shine when he notices how the excretion surges forward in small, unhurried tides up his fingers. It coats his hands like gloves, a dull energy pulsing from it.

He cannot deny the strange scent on the air. Sweat and fury and something more…a sweet, fragrant scent like over-ripe apples. It clings to the hair of his nostrils the way the gold-yellow fluid clings to his hands. It sinks into his lungs and they ache as its glory unfolds. The fury startles him a moment, just like the hiss. But coated like this, with his divine gloves, Thomas knows it is no more than a friendly watchdog for him—perhaps not a watchdog at all. If he thinks about it, closes his eyes and feels the wet pull of the divine gloves creeping up to his wrists, it feels like fury at being bound by such a fragile mortal form. The sweat, an impassioned demand from the master himself, begging release.

The master would prefer you never dared.

A laugh rings out of Thomas, childish and pure, at the wonder and majesty of it all.

With his divine fluid gloves, he reaches for the severed skull cap. It lifts off with remarkable ease now the skull has been fractured around the full circumference. A cry pulls out of Thomas as the shining excretion spills out in plush, creeping drops that just keep coming.

And coming.

And coming.

I will never stop coming.

At a volume that far exceeds the corpse that contained it. Thomas chuckles as it floods out and coats the entirety of the room.

"Magnificent!" A wavy laugh floods out of him. There is so much fluid he can't see the brain. For one horrifying moment, Thomas worries it might not be there. What if it all turned into sentient sludge and slipped right through his fingers? That would be most wretched and unfair. He clears the excretion away with his hands.

Faster.

Faster.

Faster.

Panic stiffens Thomas' movements. The fluid expands, coating things quicker than he can clear them. The source of greatness slips out of reach.

But then all at once, there it is.

The brain of a genius.

Thomas lifts it out and more shimmery goop oozes out. Heavy drops splatter, like huge, fallen water balloons onto the floor.

"Mr. Harvey? I know you said not to disturb you, but I heard a yell and—" the words die on the pretty nurse's lips.

"Don't be startled my dear, it's quite alright." Thomas holds out the brain where she can see it in the harsh fluorescent light. "Magnificent, isn't it? Unlike anything the world has seen! Of course, somebody will have to clean all this up." Thomas lifts his foot with effort. He shakes his head in wonder at the excretion which has coated the entirety of the floor. It's slowly creeping up his ankles now. "You will do nicely since you are here, my dear. Clean it up—but do not under any circumstances throw any of it away."

The nurse's brow pinches at the center. "Throw any of what away?"

She can't stop looking at the brain in his hands with wide frenzied eyes. She probably wants it for herself. The treasury of Einstein's genius.

"You just focus those pretty eyes on the mess on the floor." Thomas reminds her curtly.

"What, mess, sir?" Confusion pinches her features.

Thomas laughs in her face. He can't help it. Of course, this simple creature cannot see the divine fluid. Why would she? If he looks carefully he can see now that, yes, the fluid is all around her too, but it does not climb and cling the way it does to him. Does not recognize her as anything more than an innocent bystander.

She is.

"Never mind." He chuckles. He sees the exact judgment on her features he imagined he would if a layman were to hear him laugh during such a task. But he is beyond caring now. For he is chosen and she is not. Why should he care for her petty judgements of something so clearly beyond her.

"You removed the brain," she says slowly.

The poor silly dear. She is clearly mesmerized by the grandeur of the moment.

"The cause of death has already been noted…" she continues, when he doesn't answer right away. What an impatient girl.

Her tone and its meaning dawn on him a moment later. Righteous anger burns through Thomas. Who is she to question him? How does she dare?

She wouldn't question a man like Einstein, he can't help thinking.

Rage shakes his limbs. But he soothes himself, paints on the calm veneer of seasoned doctor she expects to see. She clearly does not possess the faculties to comprehend his excitement. It is why the fluid has not anointed her steps. She is not worthy as he. She does not deserve to see.

"Well my dear, it is the brain of a genius after all. It must be studied."

You will never stop studying it.

He smiles sweetly at her. That smile usually sends people like her on their way with smiles of their own. But she isn't smiling. She really is the most basic of them all.

"Albert's wishes were to be cremated."

"And so he shall." Thomas bites down the scream of fury he longs to unleash.

"I will inform the family the autopsy is complete shortly," she says crisply.

How dare she!

"I would have it no other way." Thomas beams.

She regards him a moment longer, then exits the room. Thomas knows he doesn't have long before she comes back with who knows what unenlightened individuals. He must work quickly.

The brain must be studied. He can't very well let them burn it to a crisp. The excretion is proof it holds secrets never seen before. It's bubbled out all over the room now. But someone else can clean it. If they can see it. And if they can't, what does it matter. It shouldn't be cleaned anyway. It is a blessing on this room. It hallows this campus.

Yes. It must stay. Thomas thinks. *But the brain cannot. They wouldn't understand.*

He packs it quickly in the red cooler his wife packed his lunch in today. There's an untouched turkey sandwich in the bottom. It makes for excellent padding with the soft bread and plastic film. A moment later Thomas realizes he didn't need the turkey sandwich padding. The yellow-grey excretion is filling up the space around the brain. Creeping slowly up the sides and rising around the organ as if someone were draining out a hose of it into the cooler.

"Well, now, well, if you didn't go ahead and make a perfectly fine padding on your own." Thomas chuckles and shakes his head.

His heart is beating faster than ever now. He knows he is about to uncover truly miraculous things about this brain. Secrets no living man has ever known. Secrets like Einstein himself uncovered in his life.

He closes up the mess on the gurney. It seems so empty and hollow now, without its power drive. He chuckles at how reverently he gazed upon this empty vessel earlier.

Plip-plip

The sound makes him turn his head. The ooze in the cooler has filled. It's spilling out over the sides. It shivers and rises up. It's shape rounded but unmistakably a hand.

Thomas frowns as it reaches for him. A flicker of doubt shadows his eyes for the first time.

"Well, that won't do."

He grabs the cooler lid and jams it on.

#   #   #

The sharp reek of formaldehyde ripens the air. Burned pickles and something dense and rotted. Thomas lets his finger traverse the wet rivers and valleys of a sizeable chunk he's been inspecting carefully. The other chunks of brain floating in the tall, glass cookie jars seem to lean forward to watch, as they always do, when he handles some part of them. The gold excretion is seeping out from the chunk in his hands. It does that whenever he takes it out of the jars; drips in huge, weepy drops that spill out onto the floor of Thomas' cluttered basement without a sound. It mostly sits where it falls, in small, shivering puddles. But some of it likes to make its way around the room. Creeping into nooks and corners. Reaching wet, yellowed fingers like stretched out webs of algae across the walls.

Nobody but Thomas ever seems to see the sticky finger webs. Whilst he's sure the slime is a blessing, he never keeps pieces of the brain out of solution for long. He can't very well have it growing over everything.

Yesterday, it grew over a pair of his boots. Thomas had tried to clear it away that time. They were his most favorite leather boots after all. And, no matter how glorious and blessed the excretion was, he didn't much like the idea of a boot-full of mystic web. He'd tried to shift it with his hands, but the moment he'd touched the wet tendrils like rotted silk, there had been a hiss and a puff of sulfurous smoke, then the webs he'd touched had sunk instantly into his hand.

And so he had noted that day, the webs did not like being moved.

The door to his basement flies open suddenly.

"What is the meaning of this?"

Thomas doesn't look up immediately. It takes him a decent moment to pull his attention from the chunk of brain in his hand and shift it to the bristling man standing at the center of his basement.

He rises from his table and blocks the bits of brain from view with his body.

"Is it true!?" the man shouts.

He blinks at the newspaper the man holds in trembling hands. The one that mentions his taking Einstein's brain for research. He blinks over the man next, unable to believe he didn't see it right away. Einstein's son. Of course it's him, but he has none of his father's greatness so Thomas feels he may be excused for not recognizing him right away.

"Well, I suppose at least some of it would be." Thomas says simply.

"You had no right! No permission—he wished to be cremated! Had no wish to even be buried, so none would come worship at his bones." The son shouts, flapping the paper in Thomas' face. "Why? Why would you do this!"

"Well…" Thomas takes a long pause hoping the man will calm if he speaks slowly. He hates shows of hysterics. "It is the brain of a genius after all. I would have felt ashamed to have just left it."

All the rage drains away from Einstein's son. He was expecting a fight, denial. He is unprepared for Thomas to be so calm and collected.

Plip-plip

His eyes follow the sound coming from behind Thomas. On the

messy table at the center of this peculiar basement lined with all manner of cadaver filled jars, lies a dreadful mess that hasn't been cleaned. A small chunk of something like a peanut chew seems to be the source the mess is oozing from.

"This is, completely beyond the pale," Einstein's son says, but there is no heat or passion to his words anymore. His gaze is transfixed by something behind Thomas' shoulder.

Plip-plip

Thomas' brows rise into his hair. *Can Einstein's son see the slime?* He wonders.

"Your father was a great man, son. A gift to humanity. His brain must be studied," says Thomas matter-of-factly.

Einstein's son's face grows ashen.

Behind Thomas the slime has risen up taking misshapen form. It reaches towards Einstein's son. "Fine. Study it, then." He gasps. He almost falls over himself in his haste to exit.

Thomas turns to see what ruffled the boy so, but the slime has already dripped back into a puddle that gives a pulse and a moan.

The sound sets his teeth on edge but he can't help but chuckle. Because even with Einstein's own son so furious with his actions, the brain chose him again.

He will study it and unlock all its secrets and become the great man he was destined to be. He will finally live up to the legacy of his father and his father's father…no, he will not live up to them. He will exceed them beyond anything imaginable. It's only a matter of time now.

He returns to the section of brain on the table. He is transfixed by the chunk before him. He doesn't notice the unimaginable volume of slime weeping from it. Or how it floods and rises behind him.

#   #   #

Shopping trolleys rattle by behind Thomas' wife but she is unmoved. She stands before a refrigerator wall packed with glass bottles of milk. A bottle is in her hand, as if she were reading its label a moment ago, but her gaze is distant now. Her forehead puckered.

It happened again this week. Thomas staying back at work. It's not like him. He's usually so predictable. Always likes his bread spread with margarine, not butter. Always has half a spoon of sugar in his coffee. Always comes home on the dot for dinner at 5:24. But not the last three weeks. Lately he keeps telling her he's busy, he has to stay back at work. Even when he is home, he lurks like a wraith in that dreadful space in the basement she wished she never agreed to turn into an office.

Something has changed. He seems…buoyant lately. Elated over nothing in particular.

Plip-plip

She's so distracted she never noticed the yellow stain on the shoulder of her burgundy winter coat when she put it on. She doesn't feel how it creeps up her neck, or when it crawls into her ear.

He's not been faithful to you.

The milk bottle falls from Thomas' wife's hands and shatters on the floor.

\#   \#   \#

Thomas wakes with a start. His body is slick with sweat. *What a dreadful, hot night,* he thinks. Chills sweep his body moments later. It's the middle of winter, he remembers. Yet his whole body feels damp. Clammy. His wife lies beside him utterly still. Too still. For a moment he holds his breath, but then—there. The gentle rise and fall of her belly. She's fine. Why wouldn't she be fine.

A pity. He can't help but think. Things might be easier if she passed peacefully away in her sleep overnight.

No. That would look suspicious after everything.

He hates how people look at him since the affair came to light. If she had just kept her mouth shut and not asked so many damned questions, he wouldn't have to bear the judgement in their eyes. Hear the whispers all over campus.

It isn't his fault the new nurse found him so interesting. And fine, perhaps he had been a little interested in her too. Well how could he not be? She said she was able to see the excretion when he showed her the brain. It was only natural they should give into their passions afterwards. The regular folk could never understand.

Plip-plip

Outside a heavy downpour has started out of nowhere. The heavens rumble with thunder.

Plip-plip

The room is as humid as the tropics. It seems to heave in and shudder out ragged breaths. Thomas longs to open a window, but the rain is hammering outside, slamming its drops against the windows furiously.

Plip-plip

The floorboards let out a low groan as a flash of lightning cracks the sky outside. Thomas' throat is in his chest at the sight of the excretion, grown in foul yellow slashes all over his room. Ribbons of it, like wet, stinking sinew stretch across the corners and the walls, over the window, up the bed and—

Someone is in the room. His eyes register for just a moment, the figure slouched over in the doorway.

"Back to bed!" he hisses. It's not like his children to come to their room at night.

Lightning cracks again.

It isn't his children.

Blobby figures of slime have gathered around his bed. Thomas presses his eyes shut.

"Soon." Thomas assures them. "Soon."

Soon…soon…

#   #   #

Eventually the slime grows too much, or maybe it's the stares. Thomas' superiors aren't happy about the affair. He loses his job at Princeton shortly after. His wife files for divorce next. It's hard for him to find time to study the brain in amidst such upheaval. He cuts a few chunks off and sends them across state in a mayonnaise jar to a scientist who studies brains. It was the easiest thing with all his equipment packed for moving. He must leave this place and all the bad luck unfolding here.

And we shall go with him…

\#   \#   \#

"Is it possible to see a slide, perhaps?"

Thomas regards the earnest reporter before him. In spite of feeling annoyed, he's slick with pride the man saw reason to track him down.

"Is any of it in Wichita?" the reporter presses.

Thomas frowns. "Um, yes. But not in the office here. Aren't you familiar with microscopic slides?"

"Yes, but—"

"Well, I don't want to say any more about it," says Thomas stiffly.

Flattered as he is, the man won't stop with his incessant questions. Prickling heat floods through him when the reporter asks why he hasn't published his findings yet.

Plip-plip

Thomas' thoughts grow sticky as he tries to think of his answer.

Why indeed? He can't quite remember himself.

"We had no urgency to publish," he says finally, feeling the need to give the reporter something. "And the actual examination didn't take this long, of course. Though there is some work still to be done. You see, my career since I did the autopsy has been sort of interrupted. I left Princeton Hospital in 1960 and moved to Freehold. And for the past few years, I've been here in Wichita. I don't work on it as much as I used to. But we're getting closer to publication."

In the end he tells the reporter the same thing he told them all. That, "It's only a matter of time now. I'd say we're perhaps a year away."

You will always be a year away.

Thomas doesn't mention how he hasn't taken the brain out of its canisters for years now. It's something he barely lets himself think on. The truth is, he doesn't particularly want the sacred excretion growing here in his office in Wichita too. He's tired of moving. And, hallowed as it may be, he can never fully accept the wet, prickling air that arrives with it.

Once the excretion grew over a house, things always became pressured, stifling. He'd left his last home shortly after that night with the storm—but that was because of the divorce. Thomas wasn't afraid of the slime, of course. He knew beyond shadow of doubt it was Einstein's great blessing to him. But like everyone else, like this dratted reporter right here, it always seemed to be asking him, *when.* When will you publish your findings. When will you explain to the world the anatomy of greatness?

"Do you have a photograph of it? Anything?"

His eyes snap up. *The reporter.* He'd forgotten he was here.

He surveys the younger man's face. There is a hunger written there that is familiar to Thomas. It is not so deeply engrained as it has become on his own features, but he recognizes it anyway.

Perhaps enough years have passed. Perhaps the excretion has slowed its flooding tendencies.

Thomas is curious himself. He's been dying to open the jars. Has yearned for a reason to extract a section of brain for inspection. The desire to touch it again, to touch greatness, is always there. Gnawing and pleading at the back of his mind.

Yesss…you must open the jars. You must touch it again.

His eyes flit sideways over his shoulder.

The reporter shifts a little in his seat and his own eyes worry over the room behind Thomas. *There's no one there.* He thinks to himself. So why is Thomas acting like there is.

"Well, I do have a little bit of the gross here." A shy smile lights Thomas' face. The words fly out of his mouth all on their own as if some unseen force moves his tongue.

A dull rattle and the heavy clink of glass sounds behind him. The reporter doesn't seem to notice, but Thomas is practically levitating at the sound. He knows what made it. It is just the kiss from the universe he needs.

No. Not the universe. Surely the spirit of Einstein himself is at work now. Leading this reporter right to his office, though Thomas has made every effort to not be found.

He knows Einstein had no wish to be made spectacle of after death. But that was many years ago. That this reporter is here now after everything must mean Einstein's will has shifted. Perhaps he now wishes to be made known. To be remembered. Thomas knows that is what he would want if it were him. The bottles themselves have rung like sweet bells.

He rises from his seat without another word. The room behind him is cluttered with boxes, papers, binders and books. He walks towards the red cooler he had back at Princeton. He's kept it after all this time. It marks a great day for him. The reporter stiffens.

Yes…it was in there for a time.

Thomas moves past the cooler and the reporter releases a small breath. Beyond the cooler is a stack of boxes. With effort, Thomas lifts a brown box sitting atop another. He's not as young as he once was and the box is heavy. He struggles with it for a few moments.

The reporter's face is a mixture of disbelief and pure excitement swelling and ebbing in rabid waves. He leans forward in his chair. Rises a little like he wants to help Thomas, then sits back down and folds his hands in his lap as if he knows he must not disturb the moment. He's been a reporter long enough to know any wrong breath can close the box as quickly as it opens. He's come too far now to lose. Finally the first box finds a different space on the floor and Thomas moves his attention to the box that was under it. The one that says *Costa Cider* on the side.

Two large canisters with yellowed masking tape around their seals sit on the office desk moments later. The very air in the room is changed. Anyone could feel it. Both men's faces glow with a strange sort of light as they take it all in. The severed chunks of genius organ trapped in time and formaldehyde.

Thomas stares at the jars long after the reporter leaves. Now that they are before him again, he can't deny how it claws at his throat to open them up. But he quite likes it here in Wichita, even if his new wife didn't want to move here to start with. He doubts she will be particularly understanding of things if the excretion consumes their home and he asks her to move again.

Thomas blinks. *When did his hand get on the lid?*

You shall release me again yourself.

His heart races as his fingers fumble with the yellowed masking tape, pulling at the lid. They move with a fervor and fury that feels not entirely his.

It isn't.

He struggles and pulls at the wiring holding the mason jars shut. It's stiff from misuse, but finally the metal lock flips up and the lid flies open. Fluid sloshes out onto his work desk. Thomas freezes where he is, then a laugh bubbles out of him. For a moment he was worried the excretion had lurched out, but it's just a splash of formaldehyde.

He leans forward, peers in at the pieces cut carefully by himself.

There's a spoon in his hand. He doesn't know when he got it out from his lunch box, but there it is. It breaks the surface of the liquid noiselessly. Captures in its concave head a sizeable chunk. Lifts the pickled brain bit, out, out, out of the formaldehyde solution.

Yellow slime erupts from the jar into Thomas' face. It floods over him, has him gasping for air. He chokes, as the excretion floods his mouth. Millions of tiny razor blades glide down the inside of his throat. He wipes out his eyes. He can't see through the gunk in his face. The slime is pouring out everywhere. A mason jar firehose out of control. It's up to his ankles now, creeping its way up his knees.

He struggles with the jar which has taken on a life of its own. Screeching out slime over every corner of the room. Finally he slams the lid back down and all is still.

But not for long.

#   #   #

The reporter releases his article and the world is set ablaze. Thomas, who was forgotten, is remembered. But not for the reasons he hoped. Everyone is in quite a flap about him having the brain. Reporters camp out on his front lawn and beg for interviews daily now. He doesn't understand what they all are clucking over. They should leave him be to conduct his research.

They will never leave you be…

#   #   #

Thomas is happy for the first time in years. He wanted to be a pediatrician all his life. Now he's a general practitioner. Finally his dream is realized, at least in part.

A woman sits with her young child waiting to see him. A strange yellow mold is growing in the corner of this waiting room. She doesn't much like the look of it. Just like she doesn't much like this Doctor Thomas, even if everyone else seems to think him the toast of the town. Honestly the man gives her the willies. Deep in thought, she doesn't notice how the yellowed mold creeps closer to her across the wall. It splatters noiselessly into her hair and feeds into her ear.

The doctor is wrong… he doesn't know what he's talking about.

"Who said that?" The woman whips her head around. But no one is there.

The woman rises from the chair and hauls her wailing child along with her. She wants a second opinion.

A new doctor tells her something completely different.

Doctor Thomas is a quack and she knew it.

Soon there are rumblings around town. After all, Thomas is an old man now. His registration dated. The board requests he takes his competency exam again. But Thomas fails.

He will always fail.

\#   \#   \#

Thomas scoops a forkful of pale scrambled eggs into his mouth. He doesn't like how the young man he's renting this apartment with keeps gawking at the jar beside him with wide eyes. His second wife never liked when he left it on the dining room table either. But she was a fool. Just like those fools who took his medical license away. Had he been able to continue his work as a doctor, he would have had the time he needed to continue his research. Instead he's been working several jobs since losing his registration. It's been a nightmare, just like his second divorce.

There will only be more nightmares.

But none of it will matter once he publishes his findings. Soon they all shall see.

Soon they all shall see.

# # #

Snip. Snip. Snip. Snip.

Thomas snips at the stream of plastic as it pumps out the extruder endlessly. The exact same motion over and over. Thousands of times a day. He misses being a doctor. This new job is exhausting and barely covers the bills.

One day he comes home from the plastics factory to find a stout man with wild hair waiting for him at his door. Professor Kenji Sugimoto has come all the way from Japan, Thomas learns. Has spent many long weeks travelling all over America trying to find him.

Thomas is stern with the professor at first, unsure what he wants. But at some point he realizes, the man isn't here to drill him about his findings like the others. Here before him is a true kindred spirit. Someone who understands.

Thomas' heart soars as he shows Professor Sugimoto the photos he has of the brain. But the professor looks troubled. Photos aren't what he's looking for.

"Uhhh…Doctor Harvey, uhhh…long time, long times in my, sah, dreams, I wish to see, ah real, Einstein brain. If possible, ahh…please ah, show me, the real Einstein brain—I came from Japan."

A long wheezing laugh erupts from Thomas' lips. "What is it you wanna see? Some of the brain?"

"Uh, yeah!"

"Okay. I have some of it left…"

"Ohhh, Okay, thank you. I wait. I wait."

"Okay. Stay right there."

"Ya, ya, ya."

Thomas leaves the room while the professor continues to thumb through a folio of brain images. Moments later Thomas struggles out with a big glass flask.

Professor Sugimoto exclaims in delight as he spots the sections of brain floating in the flask.

"He-he-he-he!" The chuckle bubbles out of Thomas' lips. It feels good to have such an enraptured audience again after all these years.

Soon three stout jars sit on the table.

Thomas frowns at the third jar. The formaldehyde has evaporated to half way. Sections of portioned brain gasp for vacant air. "This needs a little fluid on it," he says sheepishly.

Professor Sugimoto isn't bothered. He clucks and fawns over the contents of the jars. Thomas looks a little lost as he stands there and waits.

"We'll get a good study done eventually." Thomas murmurs, he isn't looking at the professor when he says it. His eyes rest wearily on the jars. "What do you want?" He bursts out a moment later.

"Uh, if ah-possible, if possible, ah, my lecture at Kinki University, if possible, sah, please ah, give me one photo, the, one piece of Einstein's brain."

Their laughs crash against each other in chaotic harmony.

"Alright, yeah, we can do that." The words fly out of Thomas' lips before he can stop them.

"True?" The professor's round face lights up.

"Yeah we can."

The professor launches in to hug Thomas awkwardly, eyes aglow.

His bright eyes dim moments later when Thomas presents him with some papers, and a picture of Einstein's brain.

"I can send you more." Thomas says, misreading the disappointment on the professor's face.

"Uhhh….if possible for my lectures at university, can you give me a piece, slice of Einstein's brain?" The professor shifts awkwardly. It's his turn to look sheepish now.

"He-he-he…well…a piece of it?"

"Mmm yeah. My long dreams, my dreams. I wish to uh, realize. My collections. Forever. My collection."

"Yeah I could give you a piece of this." Again, the words fly easily from Thomas' mouth. His body moves quickly for his eighty-odd years.

A camera crew is recording his every move for the documentary professor Sugimoto is starring in about his search for Einstein's brain. Thomas' chest puffs with pride as the crew follow him into the kitchen. He makes special effort not to look into the camera as he picks up the knife and wooden cutting board from the cluttered bench in his small kitchen. He wants to seem natural. He isn't ashamed of the mess on the bench. A messy home is the sign of a fertile mind after all.

His steps are brisk. He's kept the jars firmly shut for many years now. But not a moment goes by when he isn't thinking about them. He has longed for a reason to open them again. The professor coming all the way from Japan is fortuitous indeed.

Thomas' wrinkled hands struggle with the smallest jar. His strength isn't what it used to be, and the wire holding the lid down is reluctant to let go. But eventually the men manage to flick it up. The glass lid doesn't lift off easily though. It's stuck as if glued. The professor's hands snake in to help steady the jar just as the lid flies off across the table.

Thomas' heart sinks a little when he notes, the excretion is not present anymore. Even if it did make itself inconvenient over the years, it has always felt like some divine sign from the master. The lack of it now makes the brain feel lifeless.

"Ohhh-kay. Let me get something to fish it out with."

Professor Sugimoto's eyes dart to Thomas, a shocked smile dusts his face. Like the smile of a child who can't quite believe their parents are actually buying them the toy they begged for in the store.

Thomas returns from the kitchen moments later with a simple kitchen fork. Silver. Good prongs. Strong. He ate his breakfast with it just this morning.

The camera crew can't help their eyes from sliding over to each other, hanging on for a minute. But they are professionals. Their eyes slide back and they continue recording as Thomas dunks the fork into the flask and fishes out a robust chunk of preserved Einstein brain about the size of a golf ball, but flat and uneven on one end.

"Cheh! Cheh-cheh-cheh-cheh!" the professor exclaims upon seeing it.

Flies appear out of nowhere. Whizzing furiously around the golf-ball chunk of brain sat leaking fluid onto the chopping board. Luckily the chopping board is wood, it absorbs enough of the old brain-tea formaldehyde to stop it leaking over onto the table.

A huge fissure runs through the pale, cadaverous chuck of brain matter sitting on the wooden chopping board from the bench. The very one Thomas cut his bread on this morning. He takes the knife he used to cut the bread, a huge chef's knife, in one hand. "Okay," says Thomas, turning the chunk of brain over thoughtfully in the other hand.

He settles the chunk back on the chopping board having decided on the correct angle.

He lifts the kitchen knife.

"Hmmmm?!" Professor Sugimoto exclaims. "May I to touching it?"

He reaches hungry fingers in to poke the brain before Thomas can say anything. A particularly noisy blowfly flicks by. The professor prods the chunk carefully, then squeezes it as if he were checking the ripeness of a peach. A small, pleased chuckle leaves Thomas' lips. His hands are quick to reach back for the chunk himself.

Neither man is wearing gloves.

The flies have doubled in number.

Thomas takes the huge kitchen knife and uses it to slowly slice a thin, clumsy portion of brain. His eyes light up when he notes the sliced portion of brain bleeds the shining gold excretion the way a cut pumpkin bleeds.

He glances up at the professor who is mesmerized, reaching for the shining fluid and rubbing some between his bare fingers. Thomas chuckles again. He was right for trusting the man then if he's able to bear witness to Einstein's great blessing.

The excretion spills out over the chopping board, rippling and shivering.

Thomas watches worriedly as huge, glistening drops of it spill from the table and scurry like rats into the dark corners of his apartment.

The professor can't help himself reaching for the piece of brain on the chopping board again. Turning it over and exclaiming in delight as some of the excretion absorbs into his hand.

"That will preserve your hands," Thomas murmurs. He means the formaldehyde, but he wonders what it means that the slime has chosen the professor now too.

He plops the large chunk of brain back into its formaldehyde pool before the professor's greedy fingers can reach for it again. The excretion has wept all over his own fingers while he was slicing it. He smiles remembering the first time the sacred gloves blessed these hands. It shivers and ripples. Pierces his skin in sharp pricks and feeds itself into his flesh through the holes it has made.

"Soon," Thomas whispers to the jars, after he's sent the professor on his way. "Soon."

Beneath his skin, the excretion ripples and shrieks. Warping his features and drinking of his soul.

Soon…soon…

Author's note:

Resources

Documentary: *The Man Who Stole Einstein's Brain* – (Initial release: May 3, 2023) Director: Michelle Shephard. Editor: Nick Hector Executive producers: Carolyn Abraham, Michelle Shephard, Bryn Hughes.

Documentary: *Relics: Einstein's Brain* (1994) Directed by Kevin Hull. Written by Kevin Hull. Produced by BBC Films. Starring Kenji Sugimoto.

Newspaper article: *The Search for Einstein's* Brain by Steven Levy - August 1, 1978.

CASTLE BRIDGE MEDIA RECOMMENDS...

If you liked this book, you might also enjoy reading the following titles from Castle Bridge Media available on Amazon or by order at your favorite book store:

The 23rd Hero
By Rebecca Anne Nguyen

ANIMAL CHARMER
By Rain Nox
Animal Charmer
Magic & Melody

Austinites
By In Churl Yo

Bloodsucker City
By Jim Towns

SOUL CATCHER
By Don Sawyer
The Burning Gem
The Tunnels of Buda

**THE CASTLE OF HORROR
ANTHOLOGY SERIES**
Volume 1
Volume 2: Holiday Horrors
Volume 3: Scary Summer
  Stories
Volume 4: Women Running
  From Houses
Volume 5: Thinly Veiled:
  The 70s
Volume 6: Femme Fatales*
Volume 7: Love Gone Wrong
Volume 8: Thinly Veiled:
  The 80s
Volume 9: Young Adult
Volume 10: Thinly Veiled:
  Saturday Mournings
Volume 11: Revenge
Volume 12: Ripped From
  The Headlines
Edited By Jason Henderson
and In Churl Yo
*Edited By P.J. Hoover

Child of Dark Water
By E.G. Rand

**Castle of Horror Podcast
Book of Great Horror:
Our Favorites, Top Tens
and Bizarre Pleasures**
Edited By Jason Henderson

Cherry Dark
By R.L. Wilburn

Dream State
By Martin Ott

Dominic
By Lee Guzman

FRENCH DECEPTION
By Janice Nagourney
A Forgery in Paris
A Forgery in Lyon
A Forgery in Marseille

FuturePast Sci-Fi Anthology
Edited by In Churl Yo

GLAZIER'S GAP
Ghosts of the Forbidden
By Leanna Renee Hieber

Hellfall
By Jay Gould

Isonation
By In Churl Yo

JAYU CITY CHRONICLES
By Chris M. Arnone
The Hermes Protocol
Necropolis Alpha

**Junk Film: Why Bad
Movies Matter**
By Katharine Coldiron

MID-LIFE CRISIS THRILLERS
18 Miles From Town
By Jason Henderson
Lost Angel
By Sam Knight
Ties That Kill
By Deven Greene

**Nightwalkers:
Gothic Horror Movies**
By Bruce Lanier Wright

THE PATH
By David Bowles
The Blue-Spangled Blue
The Deepest Green

SURF MYSTIC
By Peyton Douglas
Night of the Book Man
Dark of the Curl

**The Thing That Happened
When We Were Little**
By Caroline Kelly Franklin

**Yesterday's Tomorrows:
The Golden Age of
Science Fiction Movies**
By Bruce Lanier Wright

Please remember to leave us your reviews on Amazon and Goodreads!

**THANK YOU FOR
SUPPORTING
INDEPENDENT
PUBLISHERS AND
AUTHORS!**
castlebridgemedia.com